Picture Perfect

Alessandra Thomas

PICTURE PERFECT
A novel by Alessandra Thomas

PICTURE PERFECT

A novel by Alessandra Thomas

Chapter 1

My fingers brushed over the rows of fabric hanging in my closet. I'd just spent the last hour pulling the heavy knits, fluttery tanks, delicate cardigans, pencil skirts, and dresses out of the boxes that had lived in the basement of my sophomore year dorm for the past ten months.

And I was pretty sure not a single one of them fit.

I'd hauled all these goddamn clothes two blocks north to my new room in the big brick Kappa Delta sorority house near campus. Just one reason I was grateful we were on the first floor.

I glanced at the clock. A few more minutes until I promised the girls we'd go out for the first dinner of our junior year—the year we'd all turn twenty-one, the year we'd be upperclassmen in our sorority, finally. The best year yet.

I ran my hand under the hem of my baggy t-shirt and against my belly. Damn, why did I ever have to take this off?

Thank God that tanks that dipped and draped in the front had been in style last year. I pulled one—a gauzy pink one that had always hung low on my hips with loose ruffles at the low

7

neckline—out of my closet and held it up to my torso.

Yeah, this would work. Definitely.

I pulled off the t-shirt, one I'd stolen from my big brother—who, at six foot one, towered over me just enough to make his t-shirts hang loosely—and threw it to the floor. I was careful not to look down at my waistline. I didn't want to see the way my belly curved and creased over my hip if I turned the wrong way. I even put on my bra over the sports bra I'd been wearing since early that morning, just so I didn't have to feel the way my breasts hung, heavy, resting against my ribs in a way they never had before.

Never before last Thanksgiving, anyway. I'd been at my dad and stepmother's for the holiday, running barrels with my favorite horse, Sloane. I'd never know why, but she'd bucked me during a run, and I'd broken my lower leg at the joint.

Three surgeries, a huge metal rod and two screws later, not to mention countless doses of steroids, six weeks of bed rest, and ten months of physical therapy, I'd gained sixty pounds and four sizes.

Sixty pounds. And four sizes.

I repeated what everyone had told me as I snapped my bra into place and shimmied out of the sports bra: Dressing was all about wearing what was best for your body. I believed that. I always had. Being a fashion design major meant understanding how to make clothes look good on all bodies. I'd pull some gorgeous boots over these stretch jeans, and this gauzy, fluttery shirt would skim right over my belly and the place where my back rolled down over my bra, no matter how thick the band was.

That is, I thought it would, until I put it on.

No, no. Nonono. Instead of flowing around my torso and hiding every bump, roll, and curve, the shirt clung close to my hips and brushed the underside of my boobs.

Shit.

I ripped it off, threw it on the floor, and tore through the closet that I'd just spent the last hour so carefully organizing. But even before I dove all the way in, tangling the hangers and scraping my arms on their wire curves, I knew. That was the loosest shirt I owned. And now it was tight.

I stood back and put my hands on my hips, my breaths becoming more rapid as I stared, panicked, into the closet.

It was not possible that I literally had nothing to wear on my first night back on campus.

The faster my breaths got, the harder it was to get air into my lungs. I pulled Max's t-shirt on back over my head, and trudged down the stairs.

I never moved faster than trudging these days. I'd be recovering for years from this damn surgery. And my legs would never again strut seamlessly one in front of the other, carrying my body effortlessly down the runway.

I headed to the kitchen. One good thing about being fat was that no one cared if you got a little fatter. They kind of expected it.

I found a half-used tube of chocolate chip cookie dough in the fridge with my best friend's name scrawled on the wrapper in permanent marker.Leave it to Joey to have baked a batch of cookies in the three days since she'd been back. I found a spoon in the drawer, plopped down on the couch in the next room, and dug in.

The rush of sugar and chocolate and doughy sweetness shot through my system. I tilted my head back, closed my eyes, and for just a second, it didn't matter that the only clothing in my possession I felt comfortable in was a ratty rugby t-shirt I'd stolen from my big brother.

Just for a second.

That's when Joey burst into the house, her cheeks flushed, her flyaway curls stuck to the side of her face with sweat. She had four plastic bags from Target biting into one arm and a twenty-four-pack of toilet paper balancing on the other.

"A little help here, Cat?"

I hoisted myself to my feet and grabbed the toilet paper while Joey blew out an exhausted laugh. "Holy shit. You don't know how hot it is until you get out there." She glanced at her phone. "At least we have like an hour till we need to leave, and I have no one to impress. Unlike you." She set the other bags down and elbowed me in the ribs—easy, because she was only five foot two next to my towering Amazonian frame. "Speaking of, have you heard from him?"

"Him, who?"

Joey rolled her eyes. "You know who. Don't even start with me. Good ol' Jakey! Mister Tongue!"

I laughed and flushed red. Jake and I had first made out February of my freshman year, at a recruitment party for my sorority when I was far too drunk and he was far too...something. The next morning I gave all my new sisters a full-on demonstration of the wet-tongue acrobatics he'd subjected me to. Those that I'd remembered, anyway.

The girls had all laughed, and immediately after, swooned when I pulled up a picture of us together at the party. He was hot. One of the hottest guys I'd ever seen—from home, at Drexel University, in a magazine, period. He was a year older, too. The most crucial part of his hotness was that he was tall—tall enough that in the following months, I'd bought all the cute stilettos I'd always avoided, and he'd gotten a kick out of easily grabbing me around my slim waist, pulling me into a corner, and doing unspeakably delightful things to me.

Too bad those stilettos were so short-lived. No way I'd get back into them now. I could barely walk a distance in any of the pairs of flats I'd amassed since the accident. Not with my damn gimpy leg and the ache I felt deep in my shin with any impact exercise, including walking from club to club in beautiful shoes. Or walking a runway.

"No, I haven't heard from him. I mean, I talked to him last week, but not for long. He's been on vacation, you know."

Joey nodded knowingly. Jake and I texted every day after my accident, and talked every few days on the phone. But the truth was, that was just at first. As the last few weeks of spring semester wore on, when he was in Philly and I was stuck at home in Pittsburgh, the days between calls had stretched to weeks. He liked sports and I wasn't moving off the couch any time soon. It was sort of hard to maintain a connection when my tongue wasn't in his mouth, or somewhere else, I guessed.

Just then, my phone buzzed.

I flipped it over and there was a text from Jake. Hey gorgeous. You coming out tonight?

My heart dropped into my stomach. My reflexes wanted to preen, but my belly rolls told me otherwise. I always loved it when he called me gorgeous.

The look on my face must have betrayed me. Joey leaned in and did a little dance. "Ooooh, what'd he say?"

I should have been excited. My body should have flushed with wanting him. But instead, a lump rose in my throat and tears stung my cheeks.

The smile on Joey's face melted away. She'd been my roommate since my first day at Drexel, and had seen me in pretty much every college-girl situation imaginable. She knew.

"Oh, honey. Oh no. What's the matter? Did he dump you?"

I barked out a laugh. "No, but he will."

"What are you talking about?

"You know all my clothes? The ones that were in storage here at the house?"

"Yeah...?"

"Well, I just hung them all up, and tried a few things on. And nothing fits. *Nothing.*"

Joey stepped back and cocked her head, looking at me. "No, you look good! We spent a whole two classes last semester learning about this.It's the size of the average American woman, and it doesn't mean you're unhealthy at all! I mean, I knew you weren't model-skin-and-bones like you were last year, but it's not like you're fat."

"Well, my clothes say I am. And the clothes don't lie."

"Seriously, though. What size are you?"

I walked over to the couch and collapsed, and felt it shudder beneath me. Awesome. "I don't even know. I've been wearing yoga pants since my last surgery. They're easier to get out of, you can roll them down instead of tugging them off, way better for physical therapy, and I never thought...I don't know." A fat tear rolled down my cheek. Shit. Now I was going to bawl.

"No. Nonono. This is ridiculous." Joey stalked over and tugged me to my feet. "You are gorgeous, Jake wants to see you," —she wiggled her eyebrows—"and so there's only one thing to be done."

"What?"

"We're going shopping."

Chapter 2

Two hours later, we arrived back at the house with two huge bags from the mall filled with jeans in my (new) size twelve, and a bunch of shirts that draped enough over my front to make me feel comfortable.

And a leg that was absolutely killing me.

I stood in front of the mirror in the outfit Joey had wrestled me into, already uncomfortable in the heavy jeans. I'd picked them because the thicker fabric seemed to suck in my saddlebags a little more, and smooth over some of the bumpier areas on my thighs. Joey had insisted that the skinny jeans were totally flattering, but all I wanted to do was yank up the right leg and scratch at the scar running all the way down my shin, already protesting against the strange pressure there.

Joey had found a sparkly gold swingy top— size large—that minimized my stomach and maximized my boobs. "Because I don't know how much you could have really gained— and I don't believe this 'sixty pounds' bullshit— however much it was, half of it went to your boobs, Cat. I'm kind of jealous."

It was the first time I'd ever really wanted to smack Joey. Even in sweats and a sorority sweatshirt, she looked adorable. And she knew it.

"I just can't believe I can't wear heels. It would stretch me out at least," I said, standing on tiptoe and then wincing when pain shot up my leg. It was like that rod in there was a Taser that shocked me whenever I tried to act like my life was normal.

I turned and checked out my butt in the tight jeans. "This is ridiculous, isn't it?"

"Ridiculous how hot you look. Seriously, Cat, Jake's gonna die. Curves everywhere." The syllables on the last word were drawn out as her hands drew an outline of my rounded silhouette in the air. She winked at me in the mirror, smacked my butt, and tripped off to the other bathroom on the far side of the house to fix her makeup. "Finish up, though. We're late," she called as she left.

She was right. I did have curves everywhere. No matter which way I turned, not a single part of my body looked thin. And when you'd paid your way through high school extracurriculars and the first year of college's room and board as a catalog model, that was not good. Not good at all.

I still hadn't called my Philadelphia agent, even though she'd been hounding me to do so all summer. I explained in the e-mails that I'd gained a lot of weight. Sixty pounds. Her e-mails back were filled with bullshit about how plus-sized models were getting more exposure than ever, and had I seen that spread in *Cosmopolitan* about two of them, and they even posed nude! And maybe this would be my big break, since now I was the same size as the average American woman, and my gorgeous face was always what got me the best jobs anyway.

Except I didn't want to be that size. I wanted to be the same size as the average me.

And I definitely didn't want to be the girl with "such a pretty face." Because everyone would know that meant I didn't have the pretty body to match.

That damn lump rose in my throat again, and I swallowed it back. "Let's get home."

Staring in the bathroom mirror half an hour later, I dusted pink, sparkly eyeshadow across my eyelids and followed it up with waterproof cat-eye liner as my insurance against more tears.

I slammed my hands down on either side of the sink and gave myself the hard-eyed pep-talk face in the mirror. "You are hot, Catherine Mitchell. You were hot last year and you have the same face this year. Just look Jake straight in the eye, walk like you're thin, and everything will be fine."

***

It took Joey and me a little longer to get to the bar than I would like. Even though it was only a couple blocks away, the uneven Philadelphia flagstones turned out to be a lot harder on my knee joint, now anchored above my leg bones with the help of some pretty serious interior hardware, than the dirt roads of the California farm and the smooth sidewalks of Ohio University where I'd spent most of the year rehabilitating. These streets were a reminder that the rehabilitation maybe hadn't been as complete as I'd thought.

I nearly sighed with joy when we saw Landmark. It was going to be so good to see the girls again, to hear them squeal over my outfit and kiss my face when they saw me. I really wanted to see the hungry look that Jake's eyes always got when they met mine. But most of all, I wanted to sit down and ease the pain in both my leg and my ego with a nice, sugary, alcohol-filled drink.

The girls had already snagged a table and filled it with six pitchers of beer and snacks. As soon as they saw us, the squeals filled the room. They grabbed Joey and exclaimed over how cute her little dress was, how they hardly ever saw her out of scrubs last year. They hugged me too, with quick, closed-lipped smiles, and an extra hard hug on their tiptoes. But they didn't say a word about my outfit. And seriously, how could they not with all the sparkles? Then, I got the head cocked to the side, and always the same question. "How are you feeling?" Nobody wanted to hear the real answer.

Someone grabbed my hand and found me a seat. I settled down, way too conscious of the way my butt spread farther than the surface of the seat and how my stomach must look from the side to enjoy my surroundings. The girls were chattering about their summers spent interning in D.C. or nannying for rich kids in Martha's Vineyard or working for their dads' businesses. All things I would have killed to be busy with, instead of physical therapy.

I tried to answer their questions about how I was doing, but it was better to just give stock answers—"Better every day," or "I feel mostly normal now," or "I'll be back in heels in no time"—than breaking down and weeping into a pitcher of beer. But the lies started to fight for space in my head with the truth, and the fight made a thick black roar that was almost impossible to see through.

Thank God, at just that moment, the bar's door dinged. And in walked three guys, headed straight for our table. And one of them was Jake.

I got up so fast that I made the table shake, and my arm shot down to steady it, hoping nobody noticed. Jake, who had been joking with the guys and wore a high-watt, confident smile, finally glanced up at me and met my eyes. And the corners of his mouth drew in. Not enough to make him stop smiling, but enough to make me notice.

Jake crossed the few steps between us and motioned for a hug, and my heart jumped. But when he drew me toward him, he had his arms around my neck, hanging loosely over my shoulders. Not grabbing at my waist and letting his fingers crawl along the hem of my shirt. Not communicating how much he wanted to grab me and kiss me, like every other hug we'd ever shared in front of my friends.

When I pressed my body against his, making sure to capitalize on my new cleavage pressing up and making a show against his chest, and turned my head to nuzzle my lips against his neck, I waited for one, two, three seconds to feel that familiar telltale pressure just below his waistband against my stomach.

Nothing.

Oh, shit.

"Glad you're back, Cat." He pulled back, ruffled my hair, and didn't kiss my cheek.

He didn't kiss my cheek. He always kissed my cheek.

Then he went around to at least three other girls at our table, all friends of ours with boyfriends, and hugged them exactly the same way.

The room spun and I suddenly really needed to put my hand back on that table. I lowered myself into a chair, and stared into the fizzy amber of one of the pitchers of beer, trying to get my bearings. Jake pulled up a chair on the other side of the table, everyone sat down, and nachos and mozzarella sticks were passed.

I was starving, but there was no way I was eating one of those.

"Whaddya want to drink, sweetie?" Joey wasn't just asking me what I wanted to drink.She was staring at me like I might spontaneously combust.

I broke my dazed expression and cleared my throat. "Nothing. I mean...uh...just a Diet Coke."

She raised her eyebrow at me. "You said you wanted a strawberry margarita. Or a Sex On the Beach.Something frozen and sweet."

"Yeah, uh...shopping wore me out. I'm too exhausted to be any fun drunk tonight."

Joey side-eyed me as she got up to grab my drink. "Okay. Be right back."

At least two other girls had seen our exchange—one of my sorority sisters, Ashley, and her friend who was visiting from out of town. Even though it was only two sets of eyes, it felt like they were all on me. Boring into me. Reading my mind, and knowing how completely embarrassed I was to be so huge, when last year I was so hot.

I plastered a smile on my face, making sure it touched my eyes, and looked up. "I'm going to the ladies' room. Be right back."

I banged into the bathroom, squeezing myself into the first stall. A sob rose in my throat as I tried to tug the stiff new jeans down, and finally I sat down, even though I didn't really have to pee. I rested my elbows on my knees, raked my fingers back from my forehead over my scalp, and took a deep breath, just like the physical therapy people had taught me to do when I needed a break. Take myself out of the situation. Take a deep breath. Try again.

Yeah, that was fine when you were in the middle of a rehab center when half the people there had it way worse than you, and all the therapists understood. Not when your hot whatever-he-was from almost a year ago waited outside at a table with a bunch of other girls, obviously not interested in you.

I sat up straighter. Even if I wanted to, I couldn't leave this bar through the bathroom window. There wasn't one, since it was attached to a damn fitness club. Just the reminder I needed. I had to get it together.

I breathed in through my nose and out through my mouth a couple of times until my stomach calmed down. I had to quit that, too, unless I wanted the next person walking in to think I was a crazy person and freak out.

Even if I was.A crazy person.

I pulled up my pants, with a little grunting and stretching, shouldered out of the stall, and stared at the bathroom mirror. Being fat required so many layers. Bra with wide band, tank top, shirt. I pulled and stretched each one back into place, trying to note which movements caused bulging or gapping.

I really should have practiced this back home instead of lazing around in stretchy pants and huge t-shirts. I just had never thought that clothing would turn out to be such an issue. It never had been before. Both in life and in the runway shows I'd done to make some cash and pay the bills, it was as easy as pulling clothes on and going. Half the time, I never even looked in the mirror.That's how sure I was that I would look good in whatever I wore.

Finally, I felt like my belly and hips were dammed up safely behind my Spanx-slimming camisole, one I'd grabbed off the rack even though Joey had grabbed a side of it in each hand, strained to stretch it, and frowned, warning me it would make me feel squished and miserable. It did, but it also smoothed things. As long as I didn't move too much.

I turned to the side and stared at myself in the mirror. Instead of a sharply defined torso and legs, I now had a body full of carefully controlled bumps.

Awesome.

That was when the tears started again. Big fat ones, barreling down my cheeks and plopping on the sink like the heavy drops that come moments before a summer thunderstorm.

Only difference was, those storms cleared the air, took the humidity away. I was pretty sure, right here and right now, that these pre-bawl tears would only make things worse. And seeing myself standing there, crying, made my lips twist down into the beginning of the Ugly Cry. Not good.

Just then, the door swung open and Joey stood there, hands on hips. "Cat, you've been in here for ten—" Then she saw me ridiculously dabbing at my wet cheeks with the one piece of toilet paper I'd brought out of the stall. "Oh, honey. What? What's going on?"

"I'm just...fat. I don't know."

She reached up to grab my shoulders, which were starting to shake with the sobs rolling up through my body. "No. No. Now stop. You look amazing. You don't look like you did last year, and everyone knows that. But you look so good, Cat." Her eyes narrowed. "Did someone say something to you?"

"No," I said, dabbing at my eyes, trying to staunch my tears like I would blood from an open wound. "But I could tell. Especially Jake."

Joey's mouth twisted down and she sighed. "He didn't feel you up like usual, huh?"

A short laugh tumbled out from my belly. "You noticed that, huh?"

"Yeah, because it was always so gross when he did last year."

Joey always knew how to make me laugh. "Shut up."

"Seriously, though. You just got back. Give him some time. I'm sure he'll be mauling you in dark corners in no time."

I peered into the mirror and tried to clean up some of the mascara that had dribbled down my face. Then I sighed, and said, "Thanks, Jo."

"I know this sucks, Cat. And I will be here for you every time. But you're not gonna be a stick figure again for a long time. Maybe ever."

"I wasn't a stick figure!" I protested. Even though I knew she was right, on both counts.

Joey scoffed. "Okay. Grab my head in one hand and my feet in the other, stretch me half a foot, and that's what you looked like. You were skinny as a twig before, and you're not anymore. That's the only reason none of your clothes fit. Everyone knows what happened, and nobody cares. But they're gonna get kind of annoyed with the whining and the moping if you don't start feeling comfortable in your own skin."

It felt kind of like she'd twisted a warm, loving knife in my gut. I knew she was right, but I still wanted the time to feel sorry for myself. But when I looked up in the mirror again and saw my careful makeup destroyed on top of puffy red eyes, I decided I was going to do my best.

Getting comfortable with how I looked was going to be tough, though, with the overwhelming feeling that all I wanted was to get the hell out of my body.

Chapter 3

Slowly, the air cooled off and the humidity left the city air, replaced by clouds of warm exhaust from buses and cars chugging through the streets. I loved to watch the sprawling city just over the bridge, and how the people moving through it changed the feel of the concrete and LED backdrop as they started wearing pea coats and carrying cups of steaming coffee. I used to love taking long walks around Philly, getting lost and discovering new murals, food trucks, and boutiques.

That was when I could walk significant distances without being exhausted and in pain.

For the most part, my classes and occasional physical therapy kept me busy enough to distract myself from a few things. Like the fact that Jake had pretty much been using me as a booty call the entire time I'd known him, and I was letting it happen. Or the fact that I was pretty broke (Mom could only kick in a fraction of my living expenses compared to what I'd earned modeling, and I'd been too stupid to save anything).Or the fact that I was depressed.

Most of the time, I felt okay. But the times when I'd catch myself staring into space, or turning down invites to go to dinner with my sorority sisters for a whole week, or wanting to sob every time I puffed going up the stairs or felt my thighs rub together...those moments were getting more and more frequent. So much so that I felt like I could bring a pillow and blanket and move into those moments to stay.

The last straw, though, came during a philanthropy event that our sorority had pulled together with another house. A simple "charity gets a tenth of the cover and food purchases" deal, to which we'd invited everyone we'd ever met.

That morning, the scale had revealed that I'd put on a couple pounds—the change in the weather had been making the rod in my leg feel funny, and I hadn't been walking quite as much. I'd also pulled a few all-nighters in the design studio, and snacked my way through them. It was no big deal, though—my sorority sisters were always bringing over something they thought would be cute on me from their own closets and lending me the clothing for the semester.

For the party, I'd pulled on some leather riding boots with stretchy skinny jeans and a long cashmere wrap sweater that dipped into a deep V in the front. Itshowed off my boobs and made it look like I actually had a waist. Because most of the girls wore heels and my boots had hardly any, I didn't even tower over them that noticeably. I felt good.

I'd just started chatting with a sweet girl from the other house, Hannah, whose sleek dark ponytail looked like a freaking waterfall compared to my messy blonde waves. She was a fashion design major too, and we were bonding over what a pain in the ass it was when people thought that all we did was glue-gun shit to pre-existing clothing all day, when her brows furrowed down and she cocked her head. "Hey, if you're in the program, how is it possible that I didn't meet you till tonight? Studio time always overlaps."

"Oh, I was home with my dad in California and then my mom in Ohio, recovering. Horseback riding accident, lots of physical therapy." My carefully rehearsed rundown of what happened to me rolled off my tongue by now.

"Oh my God, you're from California?"

"Um...yeah, I—"

"I wonder if you know my friend. I mean, it's a longshot, but—Nate, come over here."

A guy with dark messy hair shouldered through the crowd toward us. He wore a dark gray button-down shirt and jeans, and when he stopped a couple feet from me, I really got a look at him.Just the way his shoulders rounded and his eyes flashed at me made my heart race a little bit. Jesus, was he gorgeous. I had just reached out my hand to shake his when Jake walked in.

My stomach twisted, since I'd asked him to come to the event tonight and he said he had to go home for the weekend. Maybe we'd start making out in public again. And maybe actually dating like normal people would follow.

I took a few steps to the door of the bar, smiling, when the girl said, "Oh, you know Jake?"

"I....yeah. Do you?" The way she said his name was so familiar, so excited, and I'd never met this girl in my life.

"Yeah." Hannah giggled, striding over to him. He met her halfway to me, his eyes darting between the two of us. Then Hannah flung her arms around his neck, stood up on tiptoes, gazed adoringly into his face, and murmured, "Hey, baby. Glad you made it."

He leaned down and kissed her, pressing his face into her and eliciting a small, delighted noise from her. It made my heart stop and drop into my stomach. Oh, God. Maybe they just started going out. Maybe....

"We've been together like a year and a half," Hannah said. "I can't believe the two of us never met before, if you know him too."

Jake spoke to Hannah, but he looked at me. "I didn't think this fundraiser was with Kappa Delta."

Oh, great, asshole. Kick me in the gut.

"It wasn't. We changed it at the last minute, because half the other house had the flu and our philanthropies weren't that similar anyway." She giggled again. "What do you care?"

Some of my sisters who knew Jake, and about my involvement with him, were watching. Hannah snuggled up against his side, threading her fingers through his.

"I don't care," Jake replied, lowering his mouth to hers. "I only want to be with the hottest girl on campus."

He broke the kiss and looked around with a satisfied smile. King Jake had conquered his college kingdom, chosen his queen, and made out with her in front of his concubine.

But I was not about to accept that. I smacked him square across the face, hard.

"What the fuck, bitch?" he yelled, clutching his face.

I used the burning hot anger in my chest to push back the tears that threatened. They'd probably come out of my ears in the form of steam. I wished they would. "If you really only want to be with the hottest girl on campus, douchebag, then maybe you shouldn't have been fucking me on the side a year ago."

Spit gathered at corners of my mouth, and everyone in the vicinity stopped what they were doing and stared at our little nightmarish triangle. Including that hot guy Hannah had started to introduce me to. Fabulous.

"You can mind your own goddamn business. You're lucky I'm paying any attention to your fat ass at all." Jake's sneer made my stomach twist.

That was it. The tears were coming now whether I liked it or not. I pushed past Jake and Hannah just in time to see her push him in the chest with both hands and screech, "What the fuck, Jake?"

On another day, on another planet, I might have had the balls to stand there and keep berating him, or even to band together with the other poor girl getting screwed over and kick his sorry cocky ass out of the bar. Maybe even make friends with the poor cheated-on girlfriend.

But my embarrassment and my hurt and my humongous body were taking up too much space as it was right now. I pushed out of the crowd and stalked home as fast as I could, trying my best to ignore the pains that shot up my leg like electric shocks but were ten times as painful. I wrenched my key into the old sorority house door with crumbling paint, sobbed as I had to wiggle it exactly right to get the door to open, and collapsed on the couch.

As always, Joey was right behind me. Ten minutes later, she was kneeling next to the couch, stroking my hair and telling me to take deep breaths.

"I'm just in so much pain," I finally managed. "I mean, I wasn't doing well before I got back to school, but at least I thought he wanted to see me, you know? From our texts and phone calls...he wanted to be with me. But I guess not even good sex overcomes being a fatass."

"First, he never just wanted to see you. He wanted a place to put his dick. Second, he doesn't not want to be with you because you're fat, he doesn't want to be with you because he is a dick. Because you're not fat. And third, from what I heard, the sex was never that good anyway."

I watched a smile slowly, carefully pull up the corners of her mouth. My head pounded, but I laughed. "What do you mean, 'what you heard?'"

"Well, you know. You're a passionate girl. I figure you'd make a little more noise if a guy was really taking care of you."

A giggle, half hysterical and half relieved, bubbled out of my throat. "Well, you know he was my first, so I didn't know any different. But you have a good point there. Next time, can you just kick out anyone that doesn't make me scream and scratch the walls?"

"If our house mom doesn't first." She hugged me tight around the neck. "What else are friends for?"

"Um...well...dragging me to a counselor tomorrow? I think I really need to talk to someone."

She sat back and looked at me, her eyes big and sad. "Yeah. Oh, yeah, babe. I didn't realize it was that bad."

"Neither did I, I don't think, until...I don't know. A couple days ago. And right now, I can't stop thinking about how I deserved that. What Jake did to me. Because I'm so fat, and depressed, and not seeing things right, and feeling so weird about everything...I don't even know what I am anymore." My lip trembled and tears brimmed in my eyes. "I just...I don't want to feel this way anymore, you know? Everything hurts."

"Oh sweetie. You know that's ridiculous, to think you deserved it?"

I nodded.

"Okay, then. Counseling center tomorrow. I didn't want to go to my nine o'clock anyway."

The tears finally spilled over into rivers on my cheeks. "Thank you," I said over and over as she hugged me.

After a few minutes, Joey pulled back. "Now that we have that taken care of, what should we do now? Compare Jake's dick to various tiny household items?"

I giggled again. "Yeah. Let's start with some chopsticks. Got the number to the Chinese place?"

Chapter 4

The white laminate high edge of the intake desk at the counseling center curved around a lower one with a secretary sitting beneath it. When we walked up to her, she kept staring at her computer screen and clicking her mouse every one or two seconds.

"You have an appointment?"

"No, she's a walk-in," Joey said, standing on tiptoe to try to get the secretary's attention.

The woman tore her eyes from her screen and looked up at us over the rims of her shining wire glasses. "We don't have any appointments today."

"This is a student alert situation."

The woman sighed and pulled a brown clipboard off the desk from the other side of her computer. The tiny silver balls of the chain that held the pen there flashed at me as it swung beneath. "Fill this out and I'll let them know."

Joey flashed her a tight smile. "Thanks," she said, in a short snappy tone that implied anything but thanks.

We settled into some chairs in the small waiting area, and Joey handed me the board.

"What is a student alert situation?" I asked while I filled out my name, e-mail address, year, major, and why I wanted to see a counselor. I bit back a giggle when I thought about filling that blank with *seriously fucked up*. Instead I just filled in *feeling down*.

Joey looked at me and smiled slightly. She tapped her forehead with her index finger. "Psych student, right? I did a little research project in the office last year. 'Student alert' is code for 'I think she's gonna kill herself if you don't see her today.'"

I gasped. "Joey! It is not that bad."

"It's bad enough that you need to talk to someone today. I don't even want to think about what you're gonna look like six weeks from now if you don't."

My mouth dropped open. "I...yeah." I wanted to argue with her but every time I thought about how much energy it took to drag myself out of bed, or smile when I went out with my friends, or thought about Jake's announcement that he was officially and finally dumping me on my fat ass and all the embarrassment....yeah. I needed to see someone.

We flipped through magazines for a few minutes before one of the office doors cracked open, and a woman in a sweater and jeans with swingy auburn hair stepped out. She held the door for a girl who looked like she'd been crying, but thanked her.

She gave a slight smile as she passed the woman in the sweater, who gave her a quick rub on the back. "See you later, Anna."

"All right, Patty, I'm going to lunch," the woman called as she started to walk to the main door of the office.

"Doctor Albright, would you just take a quick look at the board?"

"I—" But then the doctor looked up at Shelly, and a serious look and a nod passed between them. "Sure," she smiled. Her eyes scanned the paper for a few seconds, and then she looked up. "Which one of you is Catherine?"

I swallowed and half raised my hand before I realized how stupid that probably looked. "Uh, me. I'm Cat."

"Do you have a few minutes to come in and talk to me?"

The woman's—doctor's—smile was kind and genuine. So I smiled too. "Yeah."

The couch was shabby and saggy, and creaked a little when I sat down on it. "Sorry about that," I mumbled.

She laughed. "No, it's fine. Does that every time."

I laughed, too. "I just thought it was because I was fat." I laughed a couple short, breathy laughs, trying to inspire her agreement. Whether I wanted her to agree with me or with my joke, I didn't know.

Instead, she just tilted her head to the side a little and gave me a courtesy smile. "Why would you think that was funny?"

"I don't know. It's easier than feeling bad about it."

"Is your weight what's making you feel down? That's what you said on the paperwork, right, that you've been feeling depressed?"

"Yeah, but I have no idea what the problem really is, you know? I mean, I don't like being fat—"

"You're not fat, Cat. You know that. Right?"

"Well, I mean, I guess I'm the size of the average American woman, but I used to be—"

"We're not talking about what you used to be. We're talking about what you are."

"Okay. Well, no. It's not about that. It's just...everything has changed." I told her about the whole ten months since my accident—my poor snapped leg bone, the surgeries, the physical therapy, how none of my clothes fit, how I couldn't even spend that long on a cardio machine, let alone go running, any more. How everyone saw me differently since I'd changed so much.

"Has anything else changed about you? Besides your weight?"

I shook my head. "I'm in the same sorority, same major. Same friends. I don't know. It's hard for me to go out."

"Why?"

"It hurts to walk, and I guess I have nothing to wear."

Her eyebrows went up. "I mean, I do have stuff to wear," I said, "but I don't like any of it. You know."

She smiled and sat back. "Sort of. I don't think I introduced myself. I'm Doctor Albright, and I specialize in body dysmorphicdisorders along with working here in the counseling center."

My whole body stiffened. "No. Hold on. I...when I modeled, it was healthy. I ate enough, I worked out. I wasn't a crazy person, or dysmorphic, or anorexic, or anything like that, I swear to you."

She nodded, putting her eyebrows up. "Oh, I know. I can tell that you are naturally very tall and have a smallish frame, and that you probably stayed very thin without too much effort. And I'm not saying you have a disorder now. But I am saying that if you don't take care of your issues with your body image, they will continue to be a plague on your life forever."

I sat back, stunned. This doctor was telling me that if I didn't deal with my issues now, not a day would go by when I didn't want to cry at the feel of my jeans tightening around my thighs when I sat, or stress over eating half a cookie.

"I'm speaking to you directly, Cat, because I can tell you're a relatively healthy girl who just had a very, very tough year. And I want to work with you to figure out how to cope, no matter your body shape, so that you have these skills in place for when things change later."

"My body's going to change again?"

"Your body will change your whole life. Rather, it could. Illness, pregnancy, stress, all can affect how much you eat and can exercise. I'm a counselor, so while I care about your body being healthy, what I care about most right now is your mind being healthy about your body."

Her assessment hit me like a ton of bricks.

"My whole identity was wrapped up in being a model. In people thinking I'm beautiful. I loved that feeling. I don't know how to get it back."

"What have you been doing?"

"Um...eating well.Or eating badly.Or sometimes not eating at all."

She gave me a gentle smile. "Okay. Emotional eating, we can deal with. Later. But now, I want to tackle the idea that your value as a person is wrapped up in your body. It's not your body you want to get back, though. It's how you felt when you were in that body."

I raised my eyebrow at her.

"Think about how it felt to be on the runway, or in front of a camera. What was that like?"

I let my eyes flutter closed, trying to remember it. The flash of the camera, the excitement of someone telling me the way I popped my hip or looked at them through my eyelashes was "stunning" or "perfect" or "gorgeous." I took a deep breath and told her. "The feeling that no one else in the world could look the same as I did right then, could make those clothes look as beautiful as I did. My body was the canvas, and the clothing was the art. My entire being was art."

She just sat there, watching me.

An intense unease twisted my gut. "I understand what you're saying. I really do. And I believe it, logically. But when my entire job, and a lot of who I was, was based on how good I looked in clothes, it's kind of hard to not judge myself like that. You know?"

"I know. Which is why I'm here to push you.To help you." She tapped her pen on her chin. "How strong would you say you are, Cat?"

"Well, I just publicly chewed out the douchecanoe who was using me for serial one-night stands. At a bar.In front of all my friends."

A grin spread across her face. "Okay. Do you think you can trust me, Cat?"

"What do you want me to do?"

"First, I want to tell you a story." She stood up and lifted her shirt. Her whole abdomen hung like a wrinkled curtain of skin, striped with shimmery white stretch marks. The area around her belly button sagged like it had a hood covering it.

"Kids?" I asked her, though I couldn't tear my eyes away from her belly. I'd thought mine was bad. This was like a train wreck.

She pulled her shirt back down, sat down in the chair, and smiled. "Nope. See how short I am? How petite my shoulders are?"

I nodded.

"I used to be a ballet dancer. I was quite a star, actually."

"What happened?"

"My mom and dad both died in a car crash."

I gasped. "Whoa. I'm so sorry. That's horrible."

She nodded. "It was. I was fourteen. And I didn't have any siblings to lean on. It was really just my aunt and me, and she was devastated too. And I didn't know what else to do, so I just ate. A lot.

"I almost doubled in weight, and by the time I lost it all, I was in college. I'd been a fat high schooler, never been kissed, and was just trying to figure out how to be normal."

"So what did you do?"

"I did what I loved again, but I did it in a way that was going to help me. I went back to dance class."

"So you want me to model again?"

"I do."

"Well, I can't. My Philly agent can't find any spots for me."

It was a lie. Maureen, my modeling agent had a bunch of plus-sized jobs for me—she said they were in high demand, actually—but I knew that if I walked back into that office and was surrounded by all those pictures of girls I used to work with, who were still long and lanky and beautiful, and I was reporting for a job for fat-girl clothes, I would totally lose my shit.

I thought Dr. Albright would drop it. Instead, she said, "That's not exactly what I meant. You told me you were strong, and I believe you. I have a friend who's a professor at Drexel who could really use your help."

"What class?"

"Drawing. She needs models."

"So I just go and sit in the middle of the room and people draw me? Okay. So you're going for the whole 'art' thing. Cool."

"Well, it's not 'just' posing though. It's posing nude."

My eyes flew open wide and panic seized my chest. "Oh, no. You don't understand. I'm not a nude model. My belly has rolls and my boobs sag. I have cellulite."

"So do most people. And for artists...the curvier the better." She waved her hand. "I'm not sure exactly why—something about fundamental beauty and curve and shadow and balance—but I'm sure they'll tell you."

I just sat there, trying to wait for the waves in my stomach to calm down and take deep breaths.

"No kidding?" I said carefully. "You really think this will help me feel less depressed?"

"No, I think the low-dose antidepressant I'm giving you will help you feel less depressed. I think that modeling again will help you feel more powerful, which will keep you from getting as depressed later. Most importantly, it will give you some of the coping skills to deal if some asshole calls you fat in a bar. So what do you think?"

All the excuses obliterated themselves in my head. It was at Drexel, and I was a Temple University student, so I most likely wouldn't see anyone I knew too well. I could put on weird makeup and leave through the back door. If I didn't like it, I didn't have to go back. I could even leave halfway through. It was a free country.

And the promise of feeling that power again was too delicious not to try it. Especially coming from this person who knew what I felt like, at least a little.

I swallowed, then nodded. "Okay."

Doctor Albright nodded and started scribbling on her prescription pad. "One for the happy pills," she winked, "and one with Professor Astor's phone number and e-mail. Oh! And one more to come see me again in a month, or sooner if you need."

I stood up and took the small square papers. "Thank you. Really."

She walked me to the door and held it open for me. "Remember, Cat. Try to find enough bravery to make yourself feel powerful. Can you do that?"

I took a deep breath, and my stomach quivered as I made the promise. "I can certainly try."

Chapter 5

Professor Astor's drawing class took place in a regular classroom in a regular building on Drexel University's campus. The building seemed to hold mostly art classes, and I passed rooms full of spinning wheels and easels, the students roamed the hallways with charcoal-smudged hands and paint-spattered shirts.

I had been thinking that somehow the moment I walked into the building everyone would know why I was there. "There's the model," they'd think. "There's the girl who needs to pose nude so she can get her shit together."

The only recognition I got was friendly faces. Maybe this wouldn't be so bad.

I found the classroom easily enough, and saw through the doorway there was just one person in there—a woman with frizzled, half-gray hair exploding from a floppy cloth hat in a way that somehow looked completely natural on her. She wore a gauzy tunic over flowing pants, and long strands of beads that clinked together as she busied herself with some portfolios on her desk. She was muttering to herself, and I had to clear my throat just to get her attention.

"You have the wrong classroom, darling, this is human form class."

"Oh, no." I said. "I'm it."

"You are...?"

"I am the human form. And I'm pretty nervous."

"Oh!" The woman threw her head back and laughed. "You must be Catherine."

"Cat," I said, nodding.

"Yes, you are beautiful," she said, tilting her chin up to peer into my face. "And a gorgeous height. They'll love this."

Over my shoulder, someone said, "Whoa, we're drawing a supermodel today, huh?"

For a split second I wondered who the hell he was talking about, until I realized he meant me.

A split second later, when I saw his face, I wanted the dull tile floor to split and swallow me whole.

I recognized him. And I wished I hadn't. It was Hannah's hot friend from the bar the night Jake snubbed me. Meaning, he was going to be drawing the nude model. Which was me.

His name popped into my head as my face flushed. Nate. The hottest guy I'd ever met.   And he wasgoing to see me and my fat rolls naked in about five minutes.

Holy. Shit. Holyshit.

He was one of the tallest guys I'd ever seen. I was guessing he was six foot three—almost a head taller than me. The hard angle of his jaw trailed down to a strong chin, and it was all dotted in a day's worth of dark stubble. I drank in his dark, sparkling eyes. That tousled mess of dark chestnut hair that made him look like he'd just gotten out of bed. The round neck of his t-shirt dipped just low enough to give me a peek at his shoulder muscles and the tops of his pecs when he bent down to set his bag on the ground.

Then he rolled up his sleeves. Even his damn forearms twitched with muscle and tendon. His hands were wide and strong with long fingers, and smudged with charcoal, and in the space of three seconds I had a brief fantasy about a trail of charcoal outlining the path of his hands across my skin.

Whoa.

"Yes, this is Cat, and she'll be our model today."

Nausea roiled my stomach.

"Are you all right, dear? There's a little room through that door," she gestured to a door behind her, "where you can change into your robe. You did bring a robe?"

"I...uh..." I just had my wristlet wallet, car keys, and cell phone.

"It's your first time? Really?" The guy had such a look of surprise on his face.

"Well, I used to model, but then I got in an accident, and had some surgery, and...it's just been a long time. I look a lot different than I used to." The words came out breathlessly, like I wasn't even sure I wanted to say them until they were already out. I couldn't believe I'd said anything. It was his damn friendly face that made me want to tell him my life story.

"Let's remember our guidelines, Mr. West? Don't ask the models questions?"

The guy flushed red and shuffled some papers around on his desk. "I'm sorry, Professor Astor. You're right."

"Thank you. Now, get your materials ready, hmm?"

Professor Astor gently put a hand on my back and led me to the door. "You, Cat, can call me Julia. You can go ahead and get dressed back there, and I'll come knock when we're ready for you."

My head spun. I'd known I was going to have to undress in front of other students my age. But the last thing that had occurred to me was a guy this hot would be part of that group. I gritted my teeth. Nate being here should not change anything. I wouldn't let his being here change anything. He was just a guy, and I was just a model. I was here to feel beautiful, to feel powerful. I was not going to worry about what one guy thought about me naked.

He was just one guy.

One completely gorgeous guy.

The changing room was actually a storeroom, with spare metal shelves full of containers of paint, boxes of oil pastels, rolls of paper, and dozens of other art supplies. In the middle of the room, in the four feet or so between the shelves, was a small area rug covering the concrete and a small nightstand where I could put my things.

I took my time tugging my leggings, boots, and socks off, then did the old trick from junior high where you take your bra off under your shirt. I couldn't deal with standing there alone with my naked self for the next five or ten or God-knew-how-many minutes while Professor Astor—Julia—addressed the class.

Even so, standing around without a bra was uncomfortable. It never had been before—I hadn't ever been small, but I'd also never needed specially designed industrial bras to keep the girls high and in place. Now, with the extra sixty pounds and my boobs going from a full C to a DD-cup, I probably could have put a pencil under each one without it dropping.

Ridiculous.

I crossed my arms over my ribs, half to support the girls and half to ward off the chill in the air.

At least there was a small window on this door, I moved the curtain to the side and peered at the students taking their seats. I counted five girls, one petite, three average, and one pretty curvy girl. One hipster-looking guy with a long beard and weird hat who seemed very bored, and Gorgeous Guy.

Nate.

I watched as all seven students took out their supplies and arranged them on the desk in front of them. Professor Astor stood at the front of the classroom, telling the students something, even though her words were muffled by the thick door. My stomach twisted and churned. "Nervous" didn't even begin to describe what I was feeling.

When she finally came to get me I followed herinto the classroom, the industrial-tiled floor a shock on my bare feet. In the middle of the room was a platform, about the height of a doctor's exam table, draped with a heavy white blanket. At the end of it was a solid black step stool, and with Professor Astor's gentle nudging, I stepped onto it.

From this angle, the platform didn't look so solid at all. "Are you sure this will hold me?" I whispered over my shoulder. A low chuckle came from the other side of the classroom.

Oh My God. Gorgeous Guy was laughing at me.

"Yes dear, it'll hold you. Just go ahead and sit. Would you like help posing?"

I shimmied out of my underwear, and watched from the corner of my eye as Gorgeous Guy fiddled with his pens and adjusted himself in his seat. Weird.

I turned away from the arc of students to pull my shirt off over my head. I'd done a lot of strange stuff when I modeled, but this was absolutely insane. Seven people the same age as me staring at my naked ass.For art class.

"Is there a way I can pose without my—you know"— I gestured to my chest—"hanging out?"

Professor Astor smiled and nodded. Thank God.

"Class, Cat will be modeling a prone pose for us today." She helped me sit down and then helped me roll onto my front. "She'll keep her arms folded beneath her head, and legs flat."

She briefly touched the top of my head, leaned in and said, "Just like a massage, dear." A couple of the girls giggled, and I smiled.

Yes, like a massage. Without the sheet. I crossed my arms underneath my head and tried to imagine I was at a relaxing massage. But the air in the classroom wasn't quite warm enough for that.

"Now Cat, go ahead and remain in this position for about twenty minutes. After that, we'll switch."

The classroom was silent except for the scritch-scritch sound of charcoal and pencil on heavy paper, and fingers smoothing lines across it. It would have actually been kind of soothing, if I weren't so naked. The only person who moved was Professor Astor, who pointed at some of the papers and nodded approvingly, sometimes doing some sketching or smoothing herself.

Lying like this wasn't so bad, actually. I knew the lines of my butt to my thighs were smooth, and nothing was bunching or bulging anywhere—except my boobs, just a little on the sides, which actually made me feel pretty sexy.

And then the twenty-minute timer was up.

"All right, class, we'll break and be back in five."

The girls walked off together talking about mundane things, like they'd just watched a documentary or learned about a geography equation. Like drawing naked girls was normal.

Because for them, it was. And I was doing a good job.

The hipster guy stalked out of the class, punching something into his phone, and

61

Gorgeous Guy Nate hurried out with a bottle of water he'd been sipping the whole time.

Good. I needed a break from looking at him almost as much as I needed a break from that pose. He was blinding.

Professor Astor walked over with my shirt, saying, "If you roll toward me, dear, we can put this on a bit more modestly." I smiled and took the shirt from her. "And then, if you'd like, you can just drape that blanket over your waist."

"Thanks," I said. "So, another twenty minutes after this?"

"Yes, and another after that. Did that pose feel comfortable for you?"

"More or less. I think it's because my...um...privates were covered up."

"Okay. So while we're waiting, can I suggest something else?"

I nodded, my stomach twisting again. How much skin did this lady want me to show?

"Just go ahead and sit with your knees tucked to your chest, dear, and your back to the students. They'll be able to get some good practice drawing the curve of your back into your bottom, and of course, your lovely hair."

I smiled. My hair did look damn good today.

So I arranged myself again, and immediately realized that sitting up straight for twenty minutes would be tougher than lying down for that long.

The students arrived back in class, and Professor Astor said, "Thank you, Cat. Actually, if you could straighten one leg and sort of tent the other over it. Like the stretches you used to do in gym class, you know." I smiled and did as she asked. She nodded, then held out her hand. "Your shirt, dear."

So I pulled it off again. Nate quickly grabbed for one of his notebooks down onto his lap, and I fought a giggle. Okay, Captain Obvious Erection. That felt good.

But now there was just one problem. Or, multiple problems, depending on how you looked at it. Whenever I sat down, my belly rolled up on itself, and so did the fat on my hips. I adjusted and shifted, but no matter what I did there were still pockets and bumps of fat in places they'd never been before the accident.

I took a deep breath. I could have sucked in my belly, but I couldn't really hold that for twenty minutes. Same for sitting ramrod straight. So I just held the pose as comfortably as I could, breathing in through my nose and out through my mouth. Thinking of my happy place.On the beach, in California.Listening to the waves rushing in and out.In, and out.

After a few minutes of that, I felt steady again, and opened my eyes. Professor Astor was standing over Gorgeous Guy's picture, with a charmed smile on her face. "It's beautiful," she murmured.

Yes. Gorgeous. Something about me is gorgeous.

Then Nate jabbed a finger at his easel. "Yeah, but what the hell am I supposed to do about that?"

Oh my God. What was he supposed to do about what? I wanted more than anything to fidget, to look, to whip my head around try to get a look at what part of me was so hideous that he didn't know how to draw it. But I knew that would ruin everyone's sketches.

She threw back her head and laughed. "Well, Nate, there's nothing I can do about that, is there?"

My cheeks flushed red and tears welled in my eyes. What the hell could he be talking about? I know I wasn't perfect, but nobody had seemed to have a problem with the last pose...Was there a huge chunk of cellulite on my ass or something? Did I have a weird zit somewhere?

Oh, Jesus, did I have a rash?

My mind raced, and I felt hot and itchy all over. When the timer buzzed, Professor Astor took one look at me and asked, "Are you well, dear?" There I was sitting naked on a table, and an art professor was reaching out to feel my forehead for a freaking fever.

But there was one thing I knew for sure: I couldn't sit here any longer. I shook my head quickly. "I'm so sorry. Can I...I mean is it okay if...Whoa, I'm dizzy."

I'd heard about panic attacks, and my best guess was that I was having one right now.

She handed me my shirt and I shrugged back into it, and I stepped into my panties, which were still resting on the step up to the table. Nude lace. Why had I worn nude lace panties? I shook my head and shimmied into them, my stomach fat jiggling the slightest bit as I did.

Oh, God. I was going to be sick.

"Um, thank you very much Professor Astor and...everyone." I managed a small wave over my shoulder, noticing Gorgeous Nate's. His

65

eyebrows were drawn together and his mouth was turned down.

Great. I'd probably fucked up his drawing even more by moving too soon, or freaking out or something.

I couldn't get into that little room fast enough. I scrambled to get into my clothes, and having to take off my shirt again to put my bra on was almost more than I could deal with. By the time I'd pulled on my boots and stuffed my arms into last year's coat like sausages, which I couldn't even button up any more, I was gasping for breath.

Thankfully, there was another door at the back of the room, which led to another classroom, which led to another hallway, which led outside.

I stepped out into the cool air and plopped myself on the huge stone stairs leading up to one side of the building, glad the length of the building was between me and the classroom I'd just escaped.

It was just cold enough that my breath made a ghost of a cloud in the blackening night air. I checked my watch. About fifteen minutes till the bus back to Temple arrived, and it couldn't come fast enough.

Yeah, this was never going to happen again.

Were there a few moments posing naked in that class when I felt powerful and beautiful? Maybe.

Was sitting bare-assed in front of a classroom of people with my fat rolls tumbling out all over the model table and having my body critiqued in charcoal form worth it?

No. Absolutely freaking not.

I whipped out my phone and texted Joey.

- **You around?**
- *In the library. Midterms are a bitch. Back super late.*
  You around?
- **Still at Drexel.**
- *How was it?*
- **Worst.Thing.Ever.**
- *What do you mean?*
- **I just....I have no business modeling anymore. It's just not something a body like this can do. You know?**

The tears started tumbling down my cheeks again, blurring my view of the screen.

- *Oh, babe. Sit tight. I'll get home ASAP and we'll talk.*
- **Love you.**
- *Love you back.*

I hated everything about this—mostly that a big part of me really wanted to feel better after doing this modeling gig. But it was just all wrong. Someone who was a model was supposed to get oohs and ahs from the people looking at her. She was supposed to make people happy. I was sure that someone with a nice body would have been eagerly sketched with smiles, thanked by the professor, and maybe even applauded afterward. I'm sure that's what Doctor Albright had thought would happen.

But she'd never seen me naked.

I was never going to let anyone see me naked again.

My breath came in big gasps and I rubbed the sleeve of my scratchy coat against my dripping nose and nonstop tears. Great. I was going to make my face all red now, too.

I checked my phone again. How had only five minutes passed?

Someone banged out of the door behind me and started down the steps. I froze like a deer in the headlights. If there was anything I didn't want right now, it was company.

I tried to stare straight ahead, but as the person came further down the stairs, the footsteps got closer to me.

Then he sat down beside me, his tall, solid frame buffering me against the light wind, and the silhouette of his messy hair and solid jaw making my heart flutter. And then drop into my stomach, and make me nauseous.

I seriously thought for just a second about going full-tilt and shoving my head between my knees until he went away. As soon as I turned my head to the side, though, that flighty plan was shot to hell, because his face was actually the most captivating I had ever seen. Nate. Again.

My mouth dropped open, and no sound came out. I tried again, my eyes still locked on his, and this time a muted half-stutter made its way from my throat.

This time, I really did give up. I crossed my arms across my knees and leaned my head there. "Oh my God," I moaned.

I waited for him to say something embarrassing, or worse yet, nothing at all. But instead, a big hearty laugh rang through the air. I looked up, my chin still resting on my arms, and managed a half-smile. "Yeah, I know. It was my first time. Hilarious."

"No, no. I mean, yeah. Sometimes the models freak out their first time. But you did a great job."

I scoffed. "Okay."

"No, seriously. And, um. I swear I never say this, okay? And I've already seen you naked, so it's not like I have that much to gain. But..."

"What?"

"Well, you were beautiful. I mean, you are beautiful. But you were really gorgeous with your clothes off. I mean, you're gorgeous now. I mean...oh God."

Now it was my turn to laugh. "Now you're just trying to make me feel better." The idea that someone would even have to try to make me feel better just made me feel pitiful. Tears brimmed at my eyes again.

"Hey, seriously. What's with the crying?" Nate's perfect lips twisted into a frown.

"I heard what you said to the professor. You asked her what the hell you were supposed to do about something. About my fat ass, I assume." The lump in my throat was so huge I couldn't say anything else.

His eyebrows furrowed over those dark eyes again, just like I'd seen them do when I freaked out and left. God, even when it was confused that face was adorable. Then, a second later, his face relaxed his eyes widened, and he smiled. "Cat. Seriously." He reached around and shuffled through his bag, yanking out the pad of paper he'd been working with. He pointed to the front. "See this? This is cheap paper. Professor Astor told me not to get the cheap paper, but I only had a certain budget for this class, and I wanted the really nice charcoals. Nicer charcoals get easier, richer shading, which makes sketches of beautiful women even more beautiful."

I closed my eyes and shook my head slightly. This guy sure knew how to talk.

"But see, the cheap paper..." He flipped to a sketch of me, sitting straight up with one leg tented in the air, my waves cascading down my back. "When you use an eraser, it basically destroys the paper. So I have this decent sketch drawn with beautiful charcoals that barely does the model justice, and now there's a goddamn hole in it."

I leaned closer. There was, right over the spot where he was trying to draw the scar on my leg.

"Ah. You were trying to get my battle wound."

"Yeah, and I fucked it up."

I smiled.

"Oh, God. Sorry. Language."

I laughed. "Please. I swear like a fucking sailor. When I'm with friends."

He smiled, and at that moment, his stomach growled.

"You hungry?" I asked, laughing.

"Yeah. I was gonna go out tonight, but I don't know."

"With who? Hannah?"

Realization dawned on his face. "Oh yeah. Yes. That's where I know you from. You're the one that....oh. Shit."

"That Hannah's boyfriend was sleeping with apparently the whole time they were going out? And dumped me when he saw me for the first time in a year?"

"Yeah. But...I talked to him. On Hannah's behalf, and on yours too, even though I didn't know your name."

I quirked an eyebrow. "Talked to him?"

He laughed. "I mean, I grabbed his shirt, and maybe growled a little bit. But nothing more. I swear."

A thrill ran through me at the thought of Nate standing up for us like that.

"But, anyway. Hannah took me to that party as a pity thing, unfortunately. I transferred here this year, and she's a friend of my sister's best friend and... yeah. We definitely don't run with the same crowd. No, I was thinking about going out by myself tonight. Exploring the city a little."

I let myself smile a teasing smile. "So not only do you not have any friends, you also don't want to make any friends?"

He nudged my shoulder with his and grinned. "Shut up. It's kind of weird. I'm on a mission to eat at every burger joint in town. It's kind of...I don't know. It's my thing."

He raised those sparkling eyes to mine again and then, for just a fraction of a second, they flicked down to my mouth, then back up to my eyes again. A warmth flooded me, and brought a confidence I hadn't felt in weeks right along with it. "I love burgers."

"Yeah?" He sat up straight. "Got a place for me?"

"You haven't had a Philly burger until you've had Johnny Brenda's."

"Well, before I let you show me around town we should probably do a formal introduction. I'm Nate. Junior in architecture here at Drexel."

"Cat. Fashion design at Temple." I smiled shyly. Introducing myself to a guy after he'd seen me naked was one of those things I'd never even imagined doing.

He nodded appreciatively, then stood up and reached down, and tipped his head toward the main street. "C'mon, we'll get a cab. The burgers can't wait."

Chapter Six

"I can't believe this place wasn't even on my
burger list. I would have never found it if it
wasn't for you."

"It's listed everywhere as a music venue.
Which it is, obviously, but the burgers could just
as easily have put it on the map." Most of Johnny
Brenda's was taken up by a stage and dance
floor, but dining tables ringed the open middle
space.

"You know, I didn't believe you when you
said these burgers were worth coming all the way
to Fishtown for," Nate said."Especially when I
saw that trashy sign out there."

"Trashy?" I said, swallowing one more sweet
potato fry. "It's vintage!"

"Sometimes I think this whole city is
vintage."

"True. Because vintage is something that's
amazing because it's old. Like, the brick front of
this building? You would never guess that all this
was inside." The stage was basic, and the dance
floor was gleaming reclaimed hardwood. The
second floor was basically a wide path of floor
circling a huge empty space in the middle—a

full-circle balcony where you could sit, eat, and watch the concerts. I'd always loved the mixed energy of the space, not to mention its ever-changing menu of local food—always with a great burger—and an eclectic mix of concerts.

From the flash of the shiny brass instruments the band was setting up and sound-checking on stage, I guessed tonight's music was a slow jazz trio. Fitting for a Tuesday night.

My friends had always hated to come down here—too old, they thought, and the music was usually weird. Maybe it was the design major in me, but I liked the way so many disparate things came together to create one of Philadelphia's best-kept secrets.

"I'm just saying. Back in California, a building would only look like this if it was carefully engineered and retrofitted."

"Mmm," I said, taking a long drink of the beer Nate had talked me into, along with the burger. "You never told me where you transferred from. You're from California?"

"Sort of. It was the last attempt at living near my dad. Spent summers with him every year since I was twelve."

"Divorce?"

He nodded.

"Me too," I said. "Dad's in California, Mom's in Ohio. But they split up when I was five."

"Ah, so you're a California girl!"

"Sort of," I said, smiling off in the distance. Now California made me think of ambulances and leg surgery.

"Anyway," he said, "I thought maybe if I picked a college near him, we could hang out as adults. Long story short, couldn't stand him then, can't stand him now." Nate tipped back the last of his beer. "Probably because I never actually spent any of my childhood summers with him. I'd get to his house and two days later I'd be shipped back off to Camp Eagle. Our most intense quality time together was writing my name in the back of my tighty-whities. "

"Yeah. The whole camp was some pretentious full-time summer babysitting service." He cleared his throat and sat up, assuming a deep radio-announcer voice. "Located in California's famed Tahoe National Forest, nestled on…"

"…the peaceful headwaters of the North Yuba river," I finished. "Yeah. That was my summer camp too."

He leaned forward, peering into my eyes. Then he sat back so quickly, his eyes flaring wide, that I thought he'd fall off the stool. "Cat. Catherine? Katie?"

"Um. I guess? Yes?"

"You're Katie. Katie Mitchell. Towered over all the boys at camp since fourth grade."

I nodded again, my mouth dropping open.

"And kissed Nathaniel West behind the shed when you played Seven Minutes In Heaven in sixth grade."

I cocked my head and looked at him through narrowed eyes. That hair, and those cheekbones, except much thinner and way more muscled....Holy shit.

Nate. Nathaniel. Nathaniel West. The fat kid who was six inches shorter than me and had to use an inhaler every time he crossed the soccer field. Nathaniel West, who I'd French-kissed on a dare behind the shed in sixth grade. Who was sitting in front of me right now, a gleeful grin on his face, and totally smoking hot.

Thank God all this ran through my head in about two seconds. I recovered my wits, closed my mouth, and said, "Nathaniel! From Camp Eagle!"

He stepped off the bar stool, still looking at me with those intense eyes, and stretched his arms out for a hug. And then, I stepped into his arms and was completely lost. Hell if his chest wasn't all solid, curving muscle, and his arms wrapped me in a cage of the same. And the way he smelled—not like beer and a second-day shirt, but the way a guy should smell—like aftershave and gum in his jacket pocket and a little beer on his breath. Which had never seemed sexy to me until right this minute.

A minute which, I couldn't help but notice, went on a little longer than a hug between old camp friends usually lasted. A hug that ended in his fingers giving me a little extra squeeze at my waist.

I looked up at him—why did I pull my head away from his chest, was I a moron?—and he stepped back, still looking steadily into my eyes. "Katie Mitchell," he said, shaking his head. "I can't believe I had to come all the way across the country to see hot Katie from camp."

Hot Katie? "Well, it's Cat now, anyway. And now you're the hot one." My hand flew up over my mouth. Had I honestly just said that?

Nate looked down at his shoes and I could swear I saw some pink color his cheeks in the dim light. My Lord, that jaw was irresistible. And that dimple—sweet Jesus, he had a dimple. How many things had I not noticed in sixth grade?"

"Yeah, I guess I just lost a lot of baby fat.And, uh…yeah.Worked out a lot in college. It's not important."

The soft sound of a jazz drum slithered through the air, and I snapped my head up, beyond happy for the interruption. "Music. Uh…" Great. Now I couldn't even speak.

"We could dance," he said softly, catching my eyes with his.

"Yeah. We should definitely do that." I reached down for my purse, but before I could get my wallet, Nate had dropped two twenties on the table.

"Oh, you don't have to—"

"No, no," he said, reaching back for my hand as he turned toward the stairs. "Where I come from, a guy always pays for the first date."

Chapter 7

On our way down the stairs, I tried to swallow the shock of what Nate had just said. He was Nathaniel West. Who I'd made out with at camp in sixth grade. And now he was gorgeous. And we were on a date.

And basically, my only other thought was this: I just really wanted to rip his clothes off. To be fair, I told myself, after feeling those pecs against my cheek it was only natural to see what kind of abs were just below them.

Oh my God. I was actually crazy. And really horny. But also, he was cute. Very, very cute. And very much flirting with me.

We got down to the dance floor just as the little jazz trio was starting to play. A low, brassy trumpet tone eased out over the drums in a slow, sleepy rhythm. Nate pulled me into his arms and started to sway. The dark of the room and the clinking glasses in the background combined with the music gave me a heady feeling. Even though I was wearing a chunky sweater and jeans and ballet flats, it made me feel like I was in one of the noir movies where the heroine has perfectly placed, gigantic curls, red lipstick, and round-toed pumps.

I felt beautiful. Maybe Dr. Albright's suggestion had worked after all.

Thank God, Nate didn't bring up the subject of camp again. Or me posing naked. Maybe he could tell that I really didn't know how to respond. He told me about why he transferred here—he could focus on a different area of engineering at Drexel, and also he was sick of his dad—and about how he'd grown out of his asthma and started running. "Didn't start quite early enough with soccer or basketball, but track and field was always looking for people at my high school. I actually did the bodybuilding thing for a year or so, and was a personal trainer my second year in college."

Well, that explained the pecs.

"I wish I could work out," I said. "But…"

"The surgery. Yeah."

My heart fluttered in my chest, but not the good kind of flutter. "How do you know about my surgery?"

"Oh." He laughed, then touched his forehead to mine, like it was the most natural thing in the world. "You know. The scar."

Just like that, my bubble burst. I wasn't in an elegant club where I was the beautiful girl and the gorgeous boy wanted me. I was a pathetic gimp with an ugly purplish-pink scar up my shin who wouldn't be able to dance too much longer without it starting to throb.

I forced a laugh. "My horse gave me a few things when I visited my dad last Thanksgiving. A broken tibia, two surgeries, and sixty pounds."

"And a piece of his mind, I guess." He didn't even flinch at the "sixty pounds." It was like he hadn't even heard it. Maybe he hadn't.

"Yes, a piece of his mind." Again, I tried to force a laugh, but I couldn't help but stare at my feet at the same time. When I thought about the accident, I couldn't help it. Sadness flooded every part of me.

"Oh, hey. Oh, I'm sorry. Cat. I didn't mean to make you upset."

"No, it's no big deal." I looked down, trying to avoid his eyes. "Things are just really different since then, you know? That asshole Jake snubbed me, and I can't model anymore, so I'm freaking broke."

We swayed there for a few more seconds, while I tried to let the swelling piano chords distract me from the spiral I was staring down at. But then something else distracted me. That familiar shooting pain in my shin that was finally catching up with me. Being with Nate had almost made me forget that I wasn't normal.

But now it all came hitting me in the face. I was suddenly very conscious of the cushion of fat on my hip that his hand caressed, and the way my belly fat bulged over the top of my waistband.

Nothing had changed about Nate, but I suddenly couldn't stand this dance floor any more. "And now," I said lamely, "my leg is killing me. Okay if we head out?"

"For sure," he said, drawing his eyebrows together in a concerned expression.

We headed off the dance floor, and when his hand skimmed the small of my back, where I knew the sides of it were plump around my spine, I walked just quickly enough to move away from it.

In the cab on the way home, Nate made comments about the architecture of the city, from the beautiful skyscrapers to the genius—or failure, depending on the area—of the highway system. I wracked my brain, fighting to pull out the names of restaurants to recommend. But most of my brain was occupied with not having a panic attack.

The crazy thing was, it wasn't anything Nate had done wrong. The problem was that being there at that restaurant, eating junk and drinking beer, and dancing with a hot guy, totally confident, like I was my old self, just scared me. I didn't know how to be the girl I wanted to be, the girl I used to be. Especially in this body that didn't look, feel, and move like it used to.

And I never would again.

We crossed the bridge over the expressway, and drove by the train station, under the arch welcoming us to Temple. I gave the cabbie directions to my place. Nate was talking about one of his classes, which I wasn't really following. And then one of his sentences ended in, "which is how I saw you naked."

Well, that certainly brought me back. I snapped my gaze to his. "I thought that would get your attention," he grinned. "You okay?"

"Yeah. Why were you…um…in that class again?"

His eyes captured mine. "I want to focus more on engineering for architecture. The beauty of a well-designed building is not that far off from the beauty of the human body." His eyes swept down over me, and I fidgeted, trying to find a way to sit that didn't make me feel…well…huge.

The cab slowed to a stop. I dug in my purse, but Nate brushed his fingers against my hand. He handed the cabbie a twenty, saying, "Keep the change."

When I reached for my handle and looked up to thank him, he'd already slid out of his seat and jogged around to my door. He opened it and held his hand down to me.

I couldn't help the smile creeping across my face. "You didn't have to do that."

"You said your leg hurt. And remember," he said as he waved the cabbie off, "this is my thing. I pay on dates."

I motioned toward my apartment and started walking. Date. He couldn't have meant it was a real date. Even though we did have dinner, and dancing, and…

"I hope you don't mind I walk you to your door. This is usually a pretty awkward moment, but since I've already seen you naked…"

"And kissed me." I smiled.

"That's right! And kissed you. What is that, like, nine years ago now?" He ran his hand back through his hair, making it stand even more on end. In that second, the only thing I wanted was to push my hands through it too. "So, no awkwardness here. For example, when I kiss you, it won't even be a big deal, because it's not like it's the first time or anything."

I should have let it happen. Should have let him lean in and capture my mouth with his. But damn me, I couldn't. Instead I had to try to be funny. "I was thinking you wouldn't take a girl out for burgers with onions if you didn't want to kiss her."

"Oh," he said, winking. "You have to have burgers with onions on a first date."

I laughed. "Okay, that just makes no sense."

"What do you mean? It makes perfect sense. See," he said, walking a few steps past me then turning to face me when I stopped in front of my place, "If I don't like you, and I don't want to kiss you, onion breath is a good excuse to skip the kiss. But if I do like you, and kissing you is the only thing I can think about, the onion breath won't matter at all."

But he didn't lean in. Didn't lick his lips, or look at mine. I could only think of one thing to say. "Well, um…Thanks." The edges of my vision blurred and sparkled. "So I guess I'll see you…"My speech stopped dead in my mouth. What the hell was I supposed to say? *I'll see you next time I'm naked in your art class, trying to keep my belly from rolling onto my hip?*

Except I didn't think I would ever go back to that art class. Mental health be damned, that was too stressful.

"I'm really glad I got to spend some time with you, while you had your clothes on. Not that I mind it when you have your clothes off. I mean…oh shit." He ran his hand through his hair again and gave me one of those heart-twisting smiles. "I'm sorry."

Sorry was the last thing he should have been. The more bumbling he did, the wider my grin got. I snuck glances at him as he stood there, fidgeting trying to shake off the sharp autumn cold that was just starting to curl through the air. The space between our shoulders was just the right distance to make me think he wanted to be closer to me, and at the same time, to make me question everything.

I glanced up at the house. Not a single light on. The girls must all have gone out or crashed early—not too difficult for a small sorority with only forty girls in the house.

A footstep would have closed the gap between us, and the clouds of our breath mingling between us reminded me of that. Something had changed from a few seconds ago, something in the feel of the space between my beating heart and his. I looked up to find that Nate was looking down at me—down at me— and into my eyes.

I'd never seen eyes so full of want before. And they were fixed right on mine. Not on my boobs, or even my lips. On my eyes.On me.

"Well, Thanks for—"

"I'm so glad we—"

Our words collided, just like our breath, ending in a cluster of soft, nervous laughter.

His eyes still met mine with so much intensity, more than I'd ever seen before.

"I'm glad you were crying. I mean, I'm glad I met you. After class. And in the class was great too, I just..."

"You're welcome." I grinned, capturing my bottom lip in my teeth for a moment. "Thanks for...making me smile. It's been awhile, and I appreciate it."

"Well, if that's what I'm good for." He cracked a grin.

"Oh, I'm sure you're good for much more than that." Nate's left eyebrow darted up for a split second, just long enough to know that he'd heard the double meaning in my words. And maybe thought I meant it.

I definitely did mean it, even if I didn't mean to say it.

That intensity was back in his eyes. His voice was perfectly steady and so sexy-husky when he said, "Please tell me you're going to let me kiss you."

A grin flooded my face before I could hold it back. I closed that gap between us with a half a step, and held my face up to his. He reached up, cradling my jaw in his warm hand. And then, his lips captured mine, moving against them cautiously and like he'd been desperate to do it all at once. The kiss was warm and soft and let me taste enough of him to drive me absolutely crazy. I'd never felt like this with Jake. With anyone. And it made me wonder if I even knew who I was anymore.

That was just it. I had no clue who I was anymore. And I loved it. His fingers threaded back through my hair as he pulled away and pressed back in for more. His breath was the best thing I'd ever tasted, and I'd be damned if the pain in my leg—as I pushed up on my tiptoes to get even more of him—would stop me. I whimpered as I let my hands rest on either side of his face, and flicked my tongue against his lower lip. His right hand dropped, and for a split second I thought he was going to stop kissing me, and that I'd probably die. But then it slipped down to my waist, clutching me there, pulling me so close that I could feel the telltale hardness right through his jeans, telling me just how much he was enjoying this. With a low groan, he pressed in, letting his tongue stroke mine, each movement making me want more.

I didn't know whether I wanted to go weak in the knees, or tackle him and strip him right there on the sidewalk.

Neither was a particularly great option, so I kissed him even harder, tugging his bottom lip between my teeth. He sighed into my mouth, and I was in heaven and hell at the same time. His lips drifted down my jaw and kissed a hot trail down my throat, and I whimpered, pressing my body into his even more.

But then, suddenly, inexplicably, it ended, and he pulled away from me. I rested back on my heels, keeping my forehead pressed against his, gasping for breath.

"That was....Jesus, Cat. You're gonna kill me."

I didn't know if he was asking to come up to my room with me, but suddenly, it was all I could think about. I wanted to feel his skin against mine, everywhere.

That was, until I actually thought about what that meant. Nate, the sexiest guy I'd ever kissed, made of hard muscle, touching my flab.

But there was something stronger, an undeniable need to be closer to him,that quickly covered that thought. I wanted him, even if it meant I had to keep the lights out and the covers pulled up. With the way he made me feel when he kissed me, I'd do pretty much anything to be closer to him.

"Don't die on the street," I managed between breaths. "Come upstairs."

A low groan escaped his throat. "Dammit, Cat."

"What? Stay."

"I can't."

All the air rushed out of my body.

And then he said:"I mean, I don't want to."

Tears pricked at my eyes for the second time that night, threatening to spill out. "Right, yeah, I get it." I dropped my hand from his, thinking for a moment that it was a shame that our hands fit so well together, that his chest felt so addictive pressing up against mine. It was a shame because I'd never be able to get it out of my head. "Well, still. Thanks." I turned to go inside, lowering my gaze. I didn't want him to see the hurt on my face, and just as importantly, I didn't want to trip on that pesky flagstone on my way in and embarrass myself, or hurt my leg, even more.

His hand caught mine. "Cat, no. No, it's not like that. I know what you're thinking. That guy who dumped you? He's an idiot." He tugged my arm gently until I turned back around to face him. "There are very few things I would like more than sleeping with you right now. But I just…can't."

I wanted to believe his words were true, but at the same time I realized they made absolutely no sense. Either he wanted me, or he didn't. The various pieces of the evening, beautiful and confusing and terrifying, swirled through my head and jumbled together in a mix I couldn't sort out. I didn't know what was up or down anymore.

The only thing I knew was that if I didn't go inside—didn't get away from this beautiful guy who claimed he wanted me but wouldn't come in—I would throw my arms around his waist, drag him inside, and not give him a choice.

So I said the only thing I could think of. "Thank you." Then I turned to go inside. He sighed deeply as I carefully made my way up the stairs. Just as I was jiggling my key in the lock, he finally spoke up. "Hey!" he called. "I don't have your number!"

I looked down at him, with his muscled shoulders slumped and his face looking drawn and sad. "If you really want it, you'll find it." And then I went inside, shutting the door on him before he could confuse me even more.

I trudged into the bathroom, washed my face, and popped four extra-strength Tylenol. I stretched out on my bed and rolled my ankle, sucking in air at the nagging, dull pain that metal rods and screws made when they were forced to live next to bones.

Why the hell hadn't I given Nate my number? I cursed myself over and over again. I hadn't loved being Jake's booty call, by any means, but I was finding out that it was kind of worse to offer to sleep with a guy and get turned down.

My life just kept getting worse and worse.

I just knew one thing for sure. I was definitely never going back to that art class.

Chapter 8

I woke up to a sharp knock on my door, and then Joey came bursting in.

"Cat, what the hell? Are you okay? Are you sick?" Her voice did the exact same thing as my mom's when she was stressed—jump up at the end into a screech.

"You sound like a damn police siren, Joey."

She laughed. "Well, so does your cell phone alarm, which has been going off for the last forty-five minutes."

I rolled over and groaned, swiping at the touchscreen on my phone to silence it. "Oh my God. What time is it?"

"Time for you to get to your ten o'clock, if you want to. Seriously, what happened to you? I texted you to see what you wanted me to bring home for dinner, and by the time I got here, you were home and passed out."

I sat up, rubbing my fingers against my eyes, trying to wipe the scratchy bleariness away. A shake of my head and some hard blinking had my head a little bit clearer. "I, um…I kind of met someone."

Joey gasped and grabbed my desk chair, spinning it around on its wheels to face me, and plopped down on it. "Oh my God. Tell me everything. How did you even meet him? Weren't you coming straight home from that art class?"

I laughed. "Okay, okay. One question at a time. He was actually in the art class."

She squealed, and I blinked hard again. "So he was in the class where people were drawing your gorgeous ass naked? Cat!"

"Yeah," I chuckled, "and he still talked to me afterward."

"Nuh-uh. That's not all that happened. Spill."

"Well, he talked to me, and bought me dinner, and brought me home."

"And?"

"And he kissed me."

Joey pumped her legs up and down and clapped her hands like one of those manic wind-up monkeys that smashed cymbals together. "I knew it! I knew he kissed you! How was it? What else?"

"Holy shit, Jo, one question at a time. It was fucking incredible. But then…nothing else."

"How is it possible that there was nothing else? Was it a polite kiss, or a kiss-kiss?"

"Um…a kiss-kiss. Like a kissy kiss-kiss."

"So why am I not awkwardly dodging this boy in the kitchen right now? You didn't want to sleep with him?"

"Oh no. I wanted to sleep with every inch of his six-foot-three, muscled-everything, dimpled self. But he said no."

"A guy? Said no? To you?"

"I'm not a model anymore."

"Oh, please. You are still a fucking model. One with hotter hips and bigger boobs and the same flawless face. Are you kidding?"

Tears pricked at my eyes. Again. *Holy shit, when was this ever going to stop?* "He just said he wanted to, but he couldn't. I don't know."

Joey leaned back, wrinkling her nose. "Do you think he has some sort of weird abstinence policy?"

I shrugged. "Lots of guys do. But I didn't get the super-religious vibe from him or anything."

"Well, you're going to see him again, right?"

"I don't know," I groaned, falling back on the bed again. "He wanted my number, but I didn't give it to him." Her eyes flew open wide and I preempted her scolding. "I don't know why. I guess I was embarrassed, or something."

"Oh, my God. Well," her eyes swept down over my rumpled clothes and hair. "It's obvious what we have to do here. You are skipping class and we're going out."

Two hours and a diet soda the size of my head later, I finally felt a little more like myself. We'd scoured the clearance racks and I'd found some cute tops that I could wear when—if—I ever saw Nate again. I ducked into the dressing room one last time, fidgeting with a weird faux-wrap top that stopped at the widest part of my midsection. I was about to announce the failure to Joey when she squealed from outside.

"What?" I said in my half-exasperated, half-loving voice.

"Hold on!" Then a second pause. "Hello, Cat's phone. Oh, hi, Nate."

He'd gotten my number. In less than twelve hours. And only knowing one—maybe two—people in Philadelphia. "She's in the changing room now. So tell me, Nate, how did you get this number? Mmm. Mmhm. I see. Well, that is impressive."

I couldn't get out of the dressing room fast enough. I yanked my shirt back over my camisole, tripped into my jeans, and shuffled out, shoes half on.

"Give that to me!" I hissed.

Joey smiled at me and cooed into the phone. "Here she is, Nate. Or is it Nathaniel?" She nodded. "Well, Nathaniel. Good luck with her. She's a live wire, but she's worth it."

"Goddamn, Joey," I whined, tugging my shirt into a better position so that my belly didn't wobble so much.

She waggled her eyebrows, covering the phone with her hand. "He likes you. Like, a lot."

I grabbed the phone, then stuck it between my ear and my elbow while I tugged my jeans up, shimmying them over my love handles. "You found my number."

"Hey, beautiful," he said.

I wanted to groan at his cheesiness—I knew it was there, knew he was sweet-talking me.

And I didn't care.

"So, I found your number."

"Yeah, I'm interested in how you achieved that."

"Let me take you out, and I'll tell you the whole story."

"Um...okay. When?"

"Tomorrow night. At six. And Cat?"

"Yeah?" I couldn't keep the smile out of my voice no matter how hard I tried.

"Wear yoga pants."

I bit my lip. "Okay. See you then." Tears pricked at my eyes. That made me cry for a whole different reason. If I could wear yoga pants to this date, maybe, just maybe I could feel sexy again.

"What? What did he say?" Joey was in my face again, as usual.

"We're going out. On Thursday."

Joey's entire face lit up. "Okay. Drop those shirts." She grabbed my hand and started walking toward the front door of the store.

"What? Why?"

"You're not gonna need a new shirt. You will, however, need new lingerie. I can feel it."

Chapter 9

Two nights later, I sat on the couch in a brand-new workout shirt, one that had a low band that cinched around my hips and ballooned up from there. My arms were actually looking pretty good, because for weeks while I was laid up in bed all I could do was watch TV and lift hand weights. And I even felt good in my underwear—we'd found a stretch cotton lace bra-and-panty set that hugged my curves and encased them in a sexy shimmery pink.

Joey had spent half an hour curling, brushing out, and arranging my hair with product, then tying it in a messy bun on my head.

"Why are you spending all this time on my hair when it's just going to be in a bun?"

"Okay, is this your first day on the job? I'm putting one pin here"—she wiggled a thin metal rod on one side of the bun—"and another over here, so all you have to do is reach up and pull these out when it's time to...you know. Va-va-voom, gorgeous tumbling blonde waves.For tumbling on his bed!" She squealed, clapped her hands, and jumped from foot to foot.

I stood up, looked at myself from both sides in the mirror, and reached up to feel the pins. "Okay. And this won't fall out while I'm moving around?"

"If it does, I'll eat my shoes. My Ferragamos, even."

I grabbed her face and kissed it on each side. "I love you, you know that?"

"Who doesn't?" Then she bounced out.

Nate was three minutes early to pick me up. Which was just fine, because I'd already been waiting at the door for ten.

I shouldered my bag, where I'd stashed a chunky cowl-necked sweater and some makeup, took a deep breath and swung the door open.

Nate stood there in a black t-shirt and black running pants with a gray stripe down the side. His eyes swept down over my body.

"Perfect," he said. "So, I know it's not a typical first date, but if you're a horseback rider, you have the...um...thighs for rock climbing." That adorable pink flush flooded the skin behind his six o'clock shadow, and as much as I loved that, I didn't want him to be embarrassed.

"Yes," I said, "thighs are one thing I have plenty of." Then I laughed, and he smiled too, his gaze flicking down my body again. I hadn't felt like I looked good in workout clothes in my entire life, but Nate certainly made me feel like one of the most beautiful women on the planet.

Doctor Albright's words echoed through my head. *Something that makes you feel beautiful. Powerful.*

"I've never done this before," I said as we walked to the door.

"There actually aren't a ton of places to climb here in Philly," he said when I settled next to him in the cab. "And I promise we'll stop taking cabs everywhere soon. It's just that the train doesn't go anywhere near this place."

"That's the thing about Philly. Awesome public transportation that takes you almost nowhere fast, because everything is so spread out." Even as I said the words, I wasn't thinking them. I was too focused on how he'd said "soon." Like this was just the beginning of us hanging out and it was all perfectly normal. Like he could see into his future, and I was definitely in it.

The cab had already made it to the highway, and I let my bag drop to the floor. "So you really are Nathaniel West from camp?"

"The very one." He looked at me and smirked. "What are you thinking? What the hell happened to that awkward fat kid?"

I shook my head and laughed out loud. "I mean...I'm sure it was just a case of you growing up."

He chuckled. "Growing almost a foot and a half during junior high and high school, yeah. Also being the fat kid for five years, getting a complex, and working out like a crazy person from ages sixteen to twenty. I was annoying as hell."

"I know something about having a complex."

"Your leg?"

I didn't want to be that girl who complained about her weight on a first official date. I knew from reading *Cosmo* that guys hated it when girls didn't eat, and when girls fished for compliments. Right now, I was thinking about exactly two things: how not to look like an idiot, and how to get him to kiss me again. Because, damn. I could not get the feel of his lips crushed against mine out of my head.

He nodded, leaning forward and threading his fingers together. He had perfect hands—big and wide without being meaty, strong without being messed up. Long, solid fingers. They were hands that you just wanted to touch you. Everywhere.

I suddenly felt very, very hot.

I leaned my head back on the seat, letting the flying lights of city behind freeway construction blur into glowing lines. "I love riding in cars like this. I always loved feeling like the world was moving around me and I was still. Like nothing could touch me. Like even though everything was changing around me, I was the same."

He smiled, reached up, and tucked a strand of hair that had fallen out of place behind my ear. Which meant I was going to make Joey eat her Ferragamos. Or kiss her and thank her twenty times, because his touch was melting me, slowly, cell by cell, starting with this one spot at the back of my ear.

If his lips ever touched there, I would die. I would actually die.

"You know, you are the same Katie from camp. I can see it in your eyes."

"What are you talking about?" I laughed. I wouldn't mention how thin I had been. I wouldn't think about how I would never be that thin, not to mention scar-free, again. Not now.

"The way you look at people. It's the first thing I noticed when I saw you, you know. Like you're curious.Like you want to know more about them, and in a kind way.Like you're just waiting to love them. And then, uh...also..." He sat up and rubbed the flat of his hand against his jaw, looking like he wished he hadn't started that last sentence.

"What?" I nudged my knee into his.

"Also, your hair. It's...it hasn't really changed. Still those gorgeous waves.Actually, when I saw current you...uh...posing, that's the first thing I thought of. Past you. I mean, twelve-year-old you. Basically, that was my first kiss, and it was...formative."

I giggled and bit my lower lip, an instinct for How To Look Sexy I'd picked up freshman year in college when various boys' hands would dance over my hip bones in crowded clubs, and biting my lip was a way I indicated that I would dance with one of them. They all understood. I was sure Nate understood, too, even if I didn't mean to do it. At least, not in a cab barreling down the SchuylkillExpressway.

My head hit the back of the seat, and I gazed outside. I didn't think I could continue to make eye contact with him without babbling, or grabbing him and kissing him. Considering I didn't know why the hell he'd wanted to stop kissing me in the first place the other night...I wasn't taking my chances again. Especially before I got home, and in close proximity to a bed.

Now that he said it, I realized that maybe he just wanted to hang out because I was someone from his past in a city where he knew no one. Maybe the combination of that and the beer goggles and the having seen me naked was enough for him to kiss me like his life depended on it, but not do anything more than that. Maybe he realized it just as he was pulling away.

"So, have you ever been rock climbing?"

"No," I said, thanking every star I saw in the clear Pennsylvania sky that he had started a new conversation. "This is going to sound stupid, but...I always thought it looked too dangerous?"

"Says the girl who got thrown from her horse."

"I know, I know. But my dad owns
        them, and it's a family thing, and I've
        been doing it
since I was three, and..."

"Yeah, I get it. I was just teasing you."

"Oh," I said, flicking my eyes to his. Jesus, he
was looking at me like he'd known me for years.
Which, I guess he had. But there was something
behind them I just couldn't define.

After a few more minutes, the cab pulled off
an exit and drove about a quarter mile to a huge
brown brick building stretched over a parking
lot. In the middle of nowhere.

Nate passed a bill to the driver and came
around to my side to open the door again. Inside,
the building smelled like rubber and sweat, and
its walls were entirely lined with gray walls
studded with colored plastic.

"Thursday nights are usually pretty dead at
gyms," Nate explained as he grabbed my hand,
like it was the most natural thing in the world,
and led me toward the check in desk. He spoke
with the front desk person for a few minutes, a
guy about a foot shorter than him but just as
muscled. Jesus, rock climbing really was a full-
body workout.

"I know my sizes, but she's never done this, so she'll need a measurement."

"Solid," the guy said, reaching out to shake my hand. "I'm Matt. I'll be taking care of you this evening."

I smiled. "Uh...thanks?"

"Wow, dude, fifty-watt smile on this one."

I didn't know if he was flirting with me or just being nice, but I instinctively moved closer to Nate, who slid his hand around my waist. And my heart promptly started pounding a mile a minute. Those hands.On my side.Again.

Now there was no way I was not going to kiss him tonight. Even if it was all me, I wanted to feel those fingers on my face, tangling in my hair.

Matt led me to a row of pegs that held various sizes and colors of wide belts that attached to what looked like garter belts, except they were adorned with buckles and rings and brightly colored plastic things. "All right," he said, clapping his hands once and rubbing them together. "What size are you?"

Of course. The absolute last thing I wanted to talk about. I broke away from Nate, walking closer to Matt and lowering my voice as I said, "Twelve. Sometimes fourteen."

"Cool," he said, sweeping his eyes down over my frame. "Yeah, you're pretty tall. Seems about right."

He grabbed a harness from the wall and had me step into it, tightening the straps around my thighs and my waist. It could have been completely embarrassing, especially since Matt didn't seem to be that much older than I was. But he was totally professional, and fast. As it turned out, the strap that went around my waist fell at the spot I was most self-conscious, and cinched in place,it actually held in the worst of my belly fat and made me feel pretty damn thin.

By the time Matt was done fixing my harness in place, Nate had finished with his own and stood there, assessing the walls. "I think we'll start on this level over here."

"Isn't she a beginner?"

"Yeah, but she's a horseback rider."

"I was a horseback rider," I corrected."He threw me during a barrel run."

Matt winced. "I knew someone who fell down a twenty-foot crevasse, same result.

Surgery?Rod and pins?"

"On my tibia, yeah.Left side."

"Okay. You're mostly going to be using your quads, anyway, so we shouldn't run into

any trouble. How's your pain?"

"It starts to ache after like half an hour of walking, but I'm mostly back to full mobility. The worst is endurance stuff, or high-impact stuff."

"Well, then, your boyfriend made a great choice. This is pretty low-impact, but it is a great way to keep you in shape."

"Keep me in shape? I haven't worked out for months."

"Well, you look good. Seriously, I bet you still have a ton of muscle to help you out. Just lead with your right leg and you should be good. C'mon. Let's see what you can do."

Matt hooked both of us up to a rope on one of the walls, anchored into place with a thick metal hook on each side, and showed me how to visualize where I wanted to go, then move my feet there first and grab second. Every time I watched my arms reach up and the muscles in them flex, they looked good. Beautiful, long and strong. I smiled to myself.

I felt pretty good, having gotten halfway up one of the walls, when I heard a whoop from about twenty feet above me. Then the wall reverberated with Nate's pounding feet as he rappelled down.

My grin was so wide I could see my cheeks pushing up in front of my eyes.

"Showoff!" I called down to ten feet below me, my stomach churning as I realized just how high off the ground I was. I bounced a little on my right leg, and my quad burned. It actually felt kind of awesome, seeing what my muscles could do after ten months of being laid up. Or of laying myself up, I realized, my cheeks burning in shame.

"You think I'm just showing off, c'mon! Race me!"

"Maybe we can start with you helping me get down from here," I smiled.

In about thirty seconds, Nate had climbed up right beside me, reached in front of me, and put his hands over the back of mine and guiding them to the straps on my harness. Right above my crotch. "Okay, so you're just going to pull here and here, and it should let you slide down."

I was not going to look over at him, into those dark flashing eyes, when I was ten feet off the ground and could crash down to it if I wasn't paying any attention. I blew out a breath.

"Don't be nervous," he said, his voice lower, sweeter somehow. "Here, I'll do it for you the first time." His hands expertly pulled and flipped at the thick knot of rope at my waist, then quickly gripped the rope above it. "Now just let it slide through your fist. Don't grab too tight, or you'll get rope burn. Okay?"

I nodded, trying not to let my eyes flutter shut after seeing the tendons in his forearms flick and the muscles there flex. Dear God.

He eased himself down the rock wall quickly, and I followed behind, foot by slow foot.

"Doin' great, Cat! Are you okay?"

"Yeah, doing fine. When I can concentrate." I tried to keep my voice light, but the truth was, the possibility of a fall, and another injury, made my heart pound. It was only when I was five feet off the ground that I realized that Nate was staring up at me, watching my progress down the wall.

Staring at my ass.

Which was bulging over a frame made of thick nylon straps.

A lump rose in my throat while I managed the last few feet. When I was about two feet off the ground, he grabbed my waist. I sucked in, almost a gasp, when his fingers pressed into the fat above the waist strap. But as I lowered myself the last few feet, he just spun me around with those arms into a bear hug, pulling me up off the ground so I was standing on my tiptoes.

"Awesome!" he said, hugging me close and pressing his face into the hair pulled back on my head.

At that moment, I felt three things I hadn't felt in a very long time: light, sexy, and strong.

"Okay," he said, letting me go. "Ready for that race?"

But just as I touched down and put my regular weight on both legs, a deep ache throbbed up from my left shin. I tried to hide my face before he saw it twisting in pain, but he was watching me so carefully he didn't miss it.

"You okay?"

"Yeah, just...the pain's setting in. This must be a harder workout than I thought."

"Yeah, this first one does take a little while to catch up to your muscles, fatigue-wise. Matt?" he called, gesturing to the front desk. Matt came trotting back over. "We're gonna call it a night."

"I saw you from all the way back there. You looked good," Matt said to me as he helped me unbuckle and step out of the harnesses. I watched my own arms grab the waist belt and ease it down. My delts still looked defined, solid. And after the skin buffing Joey had insisted on before this date, the skin there was flawless. There were no rough patches, and it was covered in velvety, shimmery lotion.

Beautiful.

I felt my back standing up straight, bringing me to full height. I wasn't even close to standing as tall as Nate. Just one more incredibly sexy thing about him. "Are you sure it's okay to go?"

"You're not feeling good, so we're going. The gym's not going anywhere. We'll come back."

Heslid his arm around my waist again, like it was the most natural thing in the world. I pulled my abs in even more, a reflex. But I felt good. Tall, and substantial in a good, tight, muscled way.

As we got in the waiting cab, I realized two things: I had desperately needed to feel strong and fit since I got back to school, probably earlier, and that Nate was directly responsible for helping me feel that way.

And that felt about twice as sexy as his hands on my waist.

Doctor Albright's words rang through my head over and over again as we cruised back down the expressway and downtown. *Something that makes you feel strong and beautiful.*

Nate.

I glanced over at him as he stared out the windshield at the wide curves of the expressway. His hand rested on his right thigh.

I screwed up every last nerve I had, reached over, and slid my hand beneath his. Immediately, his fingers laced with mine, and he looked up at me with a gentle, closed-mouth smile. We rode another mile or so in silence, and then I turned my head to his, opening my mouth and saying, "Thanks for taking me," at the exact same moment he looked at me and asked, "How's your leg?"

We laughed as the driver pulled off at the exit nearest 30th Street station, and I smiled at the solid building lit up so beautifully.

Sometimes, I loved to go in to the train station during a free hour just to think, and always imagined how romantic it would be just to while away some hours there with someone I loved. But I hadn't loved anyone in a long time, maybe ever. I remembered one instance when I thought I'd loved Jake, one night when the sex had been good, and he had almost made me come. Almost, I remembered thinking. Next time, for sure.

But then I'd broken my leg. And then I'd gotten fat. And then he hadn't wanted anything else to do with me.

Nate cleared his throat beside me, and asked again, softer, "How's your leg?"

I managed half a laugh. "Well, it really was a workout. But you're right. I feel good. Throbbing shin and all."

"Aw, shit." He looked over at me with a concerned expression. "Do you want me to take you home?"

"Weren't you going to do that anyway?"

"Well, I...I don't know. I mean...I made dinner. At my place."

I arched one eyebrow up and gave him a little smile. "At your place?" I repeated.

"I mean...I know it's kind of forward, but you did ask me up to your place a couple nights ago, and I found this really good recipe, and I thought...I wanted to have somewhere you could put your feet up. After the climbing. I thought about this a lot, okay? I called Hannah, who called Joey, who gave me your number."

Oh. So Joey engineered all this, sort of. I had to give her credit. The girl was sneaky, and smart.

"She told me you'd been feeling like shit, about the accident, and how you used to look, and I told her I didn't get it, and then she told me you thought you were fat, which I really didn't get, but..."

"Oh my God. Okay. Stop right there. I...yeah. I've gained weight. And I kind of hate it. But I am not the kind of girl who talks about it." At least, I didn't want to be that girl. Not anymore, anyway.

"But," he interrupted, "she said to help you do something that makes you feel strong, and beautiful. So I thought, rock climbing. And then I thought, she'll feel so good that she'll eat this mac and cheese that I'm really good at making, and..."

I groaned. "Shit, Nate. Shit. I'm sorry."

"What? Too unhealthy? It's cool, I can..."

"No. Lactose intolerant. All that cheese and cream...you would not want to be near me after eating that."

"Which is why I should have asked Joey about that, too." He ran his hand back through my hair and looked at me with crinkled eyebrows. "I'm so sorry."

"No, no!" I laughed. "No, that's ridiculous. I'm so messed up." I tried to pull my hand away, because...I didn't know why. It just felt weird now, for some reason.

But he held on firmly, running his thumb over the back of mine. "No. You are perfect."

We wound through the streets, pulling up at a block of older brick rowhouses near Drexel University.

I was perfect. I tried to still my heart fluttering like wild in my chest. "Is this your place?" I asked as the car slowed and stopped.

"Yeah." That same soft smile was back. God, I wanted to jump on him right there. If I thought I could fit between him and the back of the front seat, I would have. "Now, tell me the truth, okay? It's okay either way."

"What?" My voice was breathy, light.

"Are you really lactose intolerant, or do you just want an excuse for me to take you home? Because it's okay either way. You don't have to come up," he said, looking down at our hands, "if this is all just...I don't know. If you don't like me, or whatever, I won't bother you any more. It's just that the way you kissed me was...incredible. Meeting you, here, all the way across the country after all these years... I didn't want to miss my chance. But if you're not interested, I'll take you home right now."

I should have asked him why he didn't come up to my place two nights ago. I should have hesitated, or been coy, or told him that I thought the kiss was awesome too, and let him make the first move. But I didn't. I couldn't. The only thing I could do was lean over, grab his face, and plant my lips on his.

So I did.

He gave a slight gasp of surprise, but then his hands were on me, too. One pushed up through the hair on the back of my head and the other clutched just above my waist, under my ribs, the one spot on my body with little enough fat to make me feel sexy. I captured his bottom lip between my lips, flicking my tongue into his mouth a little bit with each pass.

He pulled away from me again, and I had the worst incidence of déjà vu I could imagine. "What?" I gasped.

He cleared his throat, slowly pulled his hands away. For a second, my heart sank, but then he popped open his door, digging out a twenty for the driver. His eyes glinted at me as his gaze met mine. "I know you can't eat the mac and cheese. But will you come up for dinner anyway?"

I had no idea what "dinner" meant at that point, and I didn't really care. All I could think of was one thing—buff guys like him weren't supposed to like big girls like me, but he seemed to, and I was going to take advantage of it.

My mind flew to Joey's obsessive "first-date prep" with me—every sort of plucking, waxing, buffing, moisturizing, trimming, and polishing I'd ever heard of, she made me do yesterday. That was the second thing about tonight I'd have to be sure to thank her for.

Wordlessly, he caught my hand on my way out of the car—no way I was going to wait for him—and tugged me up the stairs. Those long, strong fingers punched a combination of numbers into a keypad at the front door, and I almost drooled watching them. Inside the main foyer, he backed me into the wall against the metal mailboxes bolted there.

His lips dove into mine, like he was dying of thirst. For me. That same warm thrill bloomed through my stomach and I had to have more of him. Had to.

Finally, I broke away, just so I could beg him, "Take me up."

"Right." His voice was breathy, deep, and made my skin almost shiver off my bones.

We walked up two flights of stairs, and I felt it. The burn of rock climbing. Suddenly, the throb in my left leg was all I could think about.

Nate jammed a key into the door to his apartment, pulled me in, and spun around to face me. But then his expression fell. "Oh my God. What's wrong?"

"Oh, nothing," I said, grabbing for his waist and kissing him again. I moaned, but it wasn't from pleasure. Goddamn leg. "I'm so sorry." I pushed away, gasping. "It's just...can I sit down somewhere?"

It was only then that I looked around at his place. A full-sized bed against one wall, a tiny kitchen in the other corner.A bathroom door beside the bed, and a flatscreen TV on the wall opposite the bed.And...that was about it. This was good news—he lived in a studio, so there was no roommate to worry about.

"Oh, my God," I said, just relieved to see somewhere to sit down. I was so far beyond pissed that the pain in my leg was aching, and starting to burn, more than anything because it was overshadowing the other type of burning I felt—the one that was telling me to tear Nate's clothes off as soon as we got inside, and mine along with them.

"I know, I know, it's not much. Just a studio."

"No, it's great. But can I sit down on the bed?"

"Of course, of course. What can I get you?"

I half walked, half limped over to the simple bed, on a simple metal frame which was completely outfitted in white sheets, topped with about eight pillows and two billowing white duvets. A sigh escaped my lips when I laid back against the pillows Nate stacked behind my head, stretching my legs across the comforter. Just taking the weight off my leg made a world of difference.

Nate didn't miss a beat. He sat down on the bed, facing me, and ran a hand over my forehead. "Are you really okay?"

"I don't have a fever," I said, smiling, but with him so close, I couldn't think about myself at all. I reached up and tugged his head forward, bringing his lips to mine again. I knew one thing as his tongue dove between my lips, tasting, seeking, playing against mine—I wanted those lips on every part of my body.

Which is why it made no fucking sense that, when his lips drifted to my neck and his fingers played under the edge of my shirt, I started shaking. And then—oh my God, not now, I begged myself—I was short of breath, and my vision blackened at the edges.

I could not be having a panic attack. Not right here, not right now. No.

I wanted him so badly. But my hands pressed flat against his chest and pushed him away.

"I'm so sorry," he said, sitting upright and running a hand through his hair. Every time he moved his arms, all I could see was the slight movement of his pecs underneath that close fitting shirt.

"No, no. It's me. I swear."

"Tell me it's just your leg. Tell me I didn't misinterpret this."

I let my head fall back on the bed. The air hit the damp trail his lips had left on my neck, and I shivered with wanting his lips there again.

"God, I hate myself," I moaned. "I'm so sorry. Just...ever since my accident...everything is so different. I feel like my whole body is just some prison for a person who looks different, who feels different. I keep trying to shake it, but sometimes...I can't forget who I used to be."

His face was so confused, and even though I'd sworn I'd never do this, I fumbled in my pocket for my cell phone. I scrolled back through the pictures from my freshman year at college, and pulled up one of me in short shorts and a tank, on the quad in between classes during the first hot August week of school. My collarbones jutted out, my thighs weren't even close to touching each other, and there wasn't an excess blob of fat anywhere.

Nate peered at the phone, then peered at me. "Skinny you?"

"Yeah," I said, looking down and shaking my head slowly. "See? That's what I used to look like."

"Well, that doesn't look like you. Not the you I know anyway."

His comment was sweet, and I knew that. But by now my brain was already a step ahead of him. I swept my hands down, indicating my whole body. "No. This doesn't look like me." A lump rose in my throat, but I swallowed hard, forcing it back down. I would not cry. Could not.Refused to cry in front ofused-to-be-fat-and-was-now-totally-gorgeous Nate.

"And when you kissed me like that...I don't know. The last person I did this with"—I motioned to the bed—"totally dumped my ass the next time he was close to seeing me naked."

He scooted closer to me on the bed, letting his hand rest on my waist. His voice dropped and he looked into my eyes. "Is this okay?"

I nodded, biting my lip. There I went again, trying to look sexy in one of the least sexy moments ever.

"I want to tell you a story," he leaned in, his voice low and husky. "About the day I went to my human form drawing class at Drexel. And instead of some ugly horny-guy model, or some old woman, or some skin-and-bones girl with ribs popping out, literally the most gorgeous individual I have ever seen in my entire life walked into that room."

"You're kidding me." My voice was a whisper. "My therapist said it was either try doing shit like that to get over my body issues, or have them get even worse."

He moved his hand farther down my waist. When it grazed against the bump of fat and skin at the top of my yoga pants, I tensed. I didn't want to hate my body.But I did.

"Did it help?" Concern flooded his eyes, laced with something like hope.

"No," I whispered, and his mouth pressed into a tight line. "But," I said, brushing my hand under his jaw, "tonight did. The rock climbing. I felt strong."

"And the kissing? Did that help?" His eyebrow flicked up, and the smile was back.

"The kissing made me feel sexy." I leaned forward and planted a light kiss on his mouth, but when his moved against mine, I couldn't stop. My breath quickened as he leaned further into me and our tongues played against each other. As my heart sped up, though, I realized how freaking confusing this must be.

"But," I said, letting my forehead rest against his for just a moment before leaning back, "It really freaked me out. And the only thing I could think about after that night was that I would never let anyone see me naked again. And it seems that applies to touching, too."

"I have a very serious question for you, then."

Oh shit. This was it. Gorgeous Nate was going to dump me, just like Jake had done. My heart sank at the same time a fresh anger flowed through me. Why lead me on, if he was just going to do that?

"Do you think that it also applies to kissing?" He leaned in and kissed me lightly on each cheek, then on my lips.

My eyes fluttered closed. A rush of warmth surged through me, chasing away the nervousness. "You know, it might not."

"Well," he said, smoothing his lips across my jaw, "I have a proposal."

"I'm listening," I said, holding back a sigh.

"I kiss you. Everywhere.Starting with your gorgeous face." He moved his mouth to the underside of my jaw, and flicked a tongue out there.

I whimpered.

"You tell me when it's too much. When you're stressed, when you're panicked, when you feel ugly. And I will stop, and we'll find something we like on TV, and we'll try again next time."

He came back up to brush his lips against mine. "Next time," I murmured. "Okay." This guy was promising a next time, despite all my freaky freaking out. Just one thought reverberated through my mind at this moment: I love you. I tamped it down just as quickly as it came up. I didn't love him. I loved the way he was treating me. He was treating me better than I did myself.

And I really loved the way he held my face between his palms, like I was the most desirable thing he'd ever seen.

My fingers drifted to the two sticks holding whatever was left of my updo in place as Nate kissed me, full and slow. I smiled against his lips as my thick waves tumbled down over my shoulders. I almost protested when his lips left mine, but when they moved down my neck, leaving a sweet, damp trail, I let my head fall back and my eyes close.

"Perfect," he murmured into the hollow of my throat, just before using his perfect hands to brush my hair from my right collarbone. He kissed every inch of it, and when he reached the strap of my tank, tucked his fingers beneath it, sat up and looked into my eyes. "Okay?"

I drew in a slow breath, and nodded. He treated every bit of skin he moved the strap across to one slow kiss, and when it finally fell down past my shoulder, flicked his tongue out against the skin there. "I don't know if you understand how perfect this line is. I spent so long trying to get it right with charcoal and paper. It's like a frame for the rest of your body."

The way he said the word "body," deep and wanting in the back of his throat, sent my hands grabbing at his back, pulling him closer. He smiled as he traced his way back over my collarbone, brushing gentle kisses over the other side as well before coming back to my mouth, licking into it like it was where he was dying to be all along. He pulled back and tucked my hair behind my ears before running his hands down to my ribs again. The feel of his fingers splayed out on my sides was almost too much, in the best way possible. "Are you doing okay?"

I nodded. I couldn't get words out if I tried.

"How do you feel?"

"Like you want me."

"Mmm," he said, brushing his lips at the corner of my mouth. "That's not the answer I was looking for." Slowly, torturously, his thumbs brushed up against my breasts. He looked at me, his eyebrows up. I nodded, fast. His hands slid down to the hem of my shirt, lifting the safe elastic band holding it in place. The same look again, testing, asking with every step whether it was all right.

The familiar pressure built in my chest, but I wouldn't let it take over now. No way was my shitty body image going to ruin this. My voice was shaky as I smiled."Yeah. But can I lie down? Get under the covers?"

He tugged the blanket from under me, and in one smooth motion, eased my body down the mattress with one arm and tugged it over me with the other. "Thank you," I whispered, and then his hands were under my shirt and against my bare skin, tugging the whole thing, including the built-inbra, off over my head.

The blanket stretched up over one side of me, and his body framed the other, and with the way his hand gripped my side, I felt solid, safe. Protected.

"Your neck, your shoulders, are the frame." He reached up and traced them, again, with his fingers. "And this is the art." His fingers traced down the side of my breasts, then trailed down my stomach. Lying down, it looked full, but relatively flat, softly curving down into hips. His palms covered my midsection, and he looked down hungrily as they moved to my sides, gripping them. "And this is where the frame ends. Absolutely gorgeous."

His lips brushed down my breastbone. "This is what a woman looks like. This is what made the masters so hungry to paint. They all knew better than the dumbass fashion magazines, Cat. Trust me. It's amazing how so many curves can all come together into something so absolutely visually perfect."

There that word was, again. Perfect. In application to me.Not only me, but my body.

He moved to my right, his body half-covering mine. I'd be damned if he wasn't all muscle. The solid warmth of his chest pressed into mine, making my breasts round and high. He covered the top curve of the right one with soft, fluttering kisses, then stopped. The breath caught in my throat and he pulled away, looking up at me again.

"Stop?" he asked.

"Please don't," I managed.

"Oh, thank God," he growled, lowering his lips to my breast again, tracing its outer edge with his tongue, devouring the surface with wide open kisses, and finally sucking my nipple deep into his mouth. I arched my back and moaned. He moved to the other side and did the same, finally kissing back up to my throat, and covering my entire torso with his.

We kissed again for what could have been minutes and what could have been hours. All I knew was that I was completely lost with memorizing the taste of him, the feel of his tongue against mine, the sensation of any guy being this careful and slow with me.

Sleeping with asshole Jake had never been anything like this.

He pulled back and let his hand cup the side of my face, brushing my eyebrow with his thumb and gazing at me. "Still okay?"

I shook my head no.

He nodded quickly, then pushed himself up and away from me. I caught his wrist before his hand left my hip. "No," I said aloud. "Would you...can I...could you take your shirt off? I want to see you too."

That was the understatement of the century.

A mischievous smile curled his lips, and he nodded, sitting back on his heels.

He reached for the bottom of his shirt with one hand, grabbing at it and tugging upwards.

Oh, Jesus Christ. Oh, sweet Lord in heaven. He was actually listening to me, to some words that had tumbled out of my mouth and into the air and now floated around my head in a halo that begged for all of him to press against all of me, all at once. Because what I was seeing now absolutely positively could never be unseen.

Abs. Everywhere. Two gorgeous columns of muscle stacked above his navel. Pecs that begged to be bitten.Preferably while his hands squeezed my ass.

Stomach rolls be damned. I couldn't stand another second of that body being uncovered and my mouth not being on it. I sat up and snaked my hands under his arms and grabbed at his shoulders, sucking at his neck and moving down to his chest. My tongue flicked out against it and oh my God, he tasted incredible. Clean, slightly sweet, with a musky smell and a trace of salt.

He moved his hand to my back and eased me down on the bed again, returning his mouth to mine. After a few seconds, I drew back just enough to murmur "thank you" into his mouth.

Before I knew it, he had pushed away again, then lowered his body even further, kissing quickly down between my breasts and over my ribs. With his gorgeous arms propping him up on elbows at either side of my hips, his breath tickled my stomach, his lips poised just over my belly button.

With how hard he felt, twitching against my knee, I couldn't believe he asked again. But he did. "Okay?" It was a low, rumbling whisper now. Like he would die if I said no.

"God, yes," I groaned, and then his mouth was everywhere, his tongue flicking into my navel and down across my hip bones. They didn't jut out sharply like they used to—now they were shadow within a curve, a soft corner marking where one thing ended and another began. Just like Nate had said.

His hands pushed my pants down my thighs and my head spun. I fought the instinct to squeeze him between my legs, flip him down on the bed, and tear his pants off. I wanted to, so badly, but I was also enjoying this way too much.

I lifted the blanket and looked down, mostly so I could watch his shoulders flex while his hands gripped my skin. I wasn't worried about his fingers digging into my fat anymore. I barely even noticed, because I was so focused on wanting more of his body against more of mine. And the way his palms pressed against me, like my curves were only helping him grab onto me, move me where he wanted me to go—I could have written my own ass a love letter right then and there.

Nate's tongue and lips were intoxicating, but when he squeezed my hip and let his teeth graze across the skin there, I almost lost it. I arched my back again and moaned.

He looked up at me, eyebrows raised. Asking permission.

"Don't stop," I gasped. He returned his lips to my body, moving down my leg.

"I have to tell you," he murmured between kisses, his voice rumbling deep in his chest. "Since the moment I watched your shirt come off in that class, I've only been able to think of one thing." He kissed all the way down to my knee. "How absolutely delicious you looked. How gorgeous your skin was." His hand caressed my calf, brushing against the sole of my foot, and a shiver ran through me. He leaned forward, pressing one hand into the bed next to my head. He kissed me again, fully, his tongue dipping between my teeth for the briefest moment, then broke away. "How badly I wanted to taste you."

I drew my leg up so that my foot was flat on the mattress. His hand played against the scar at the front of my shin, and I made a face. "I hate that thing."

He sat up, stroked the back of my calf, and lifted my leg to his mouth, kissing it gently. "Stop that. It's one of my favorite things. It shows me how strong you are." His hand brushed up along the outside of my thigh. "And I know it's responsible for this gorgeous body of yours."

Which I also hated. Until Nate looked at it and worshiped it like it was an actual masterpiece. Until he showed me how strong I could be. Now it didn't seem so bad, not at all.

He lowered himself down over me again, kissing me and smiling. "I didn't think you'd let me kiss you this much." His hand gripped my waist again, and the only sound I could get out was "Mmmm."

He moved lower again, his fingers playing a slow piano tune down my stomach, over my hips, and then between my legs.

The sensation of those fingers moving over my most sensitive area shot through me, forcing my head back, exposing my neck to his nibbles and licks. He didn't have to ask, but he did.

"Okay?"

It was the definition of okay. Unfortunately, I didn't have one syllable of all the words I needed, so I just gasped and nodded, and then he lowered down again. My legs fell to the sides, looking long and strong and actually kind of pretty. His hands reached under my ass and his lips showered soft, worshipful attention on the very spot that ached for it most. Finally, his tongue pushed inside me, and the incredible warmth and restlessness and need of it all was almost too much to bear, until suddenly it was too much to bear, and the orgasm ripped through my body in hot, lingering waves.

I laid back, gasping. "God, Nate."

He settled back down beside me, kissing my cheekbones, the angle of my jaw, the skin behind my ear. He pressed his lips up against it and his hot breath swirled through my hair. "Mission accomplished. I thought it would take me way longer than that."

I turned and lazily kissed his forehead. "To what? Taste me?" I couldn't believe the words were coming out of my mouth. I'd never talked about my own body explicitly—never even thought about it that way. Even with Jake. Especially with Jake.

"To let me kiss you everywhere." He winked, and the slightest hint of a dimple flashed in his cheek.

I thought I would die. "Oh, I'm sure there are more places you could kiss me. And I'll let you, next time. But right now, there issomething I want."

My fingers pushed under the waistband of his pants, and wasted no time drifting to the front. Yeah, he definitely wanted me as badly as I wanted him.

He closed his eyes and rolled to his back, pushing his pants down and giving me a full view. The hard cut of his abs continued in a solid path down past his hips, the firm lines of his thighs framing his own complete and total hard-as-a-rock, standing-at-attention gorgeousness.

"You have to be kidding me," I said. "You are human, right? How is it possible that your body is this perfect?"

My hands were like a magnet to his skin, and they set to work tracing every hard bit of it, my fingers dancing along his length and flicking at the head. A strangled moan escaped his throat, and I grinned like a fool.

"Do you have something?" I asked. "I'm on the pill, but..."

He licked his lips, swallowed hard, and nodded. He pulled a small square box from his nightstand and ripped the cardboard strip off of it. An unopened box, and just a three-pack at that. A just-in-case box, not an I-do-this-all-the-time box. I ticked my eyebrow up and smirked in satisfaction. A guy this hot, and I was the one girl, it seemed, he had brought home.

It was my turn for my hands to grab at his hips, for my arms to pull his body to my mouth. My lips covered the place where his shoulder met his neck, and I sucked hard. He groaned, settled between my legs and rocked into me, reaching up to brush the hair away from my face and resting his forehead against mine.

My world exploded into swirling color and heavy breaths and nothingness as my skin drank in every bit of his.

Chapter 10

Afterwards, we laid facing each other, our shoulders pressed together as my fingers trailed down the paths carved by muscle his back. His hand rested on the back of my hip which, freed from fabric and weird sitting positions, curved down into my waist without a single roll.

I was happy.

"I like this," I murmured.

"Being here with me?"

I kissed him lazily. "That too. But...I don't know. Lying here, like this, I feel like a model."

"What does that even mean, when you say that?"

"Well, when I would do a photo shoot, the clothes would just look absolutely incredible on me. They'd be loose, even. I wore some things that I still drool over. They were masterpieces."

"Fashion design major. Got it," he nodded.

"Right. My body made these clothes everything they were supposed to be. It was this tremendous feeling of power, you know? That these clothes were designed with such care, such attention to detail, but my body was the only thing that could make them into everything the artist imagined."

"How much did you weigh?" Nate asked as his hand grazed the back of my thigh and played at the back of my knee.

"I was at one-twenty, and I think it was only that much because I've always had these shoulders and arms."

"You mean, the beautifully toned ones?"

I blushed. "I always thought I was a better rider when my upper body was strong—that I'd be able to handle the barrels and the jumps better. Guess that wasn't quite true. Anyway, that was why so many of the designers asked for me. I was unique as a subset of their definition of perfect. And now...."

"....Now you're my entire definition of perfect."

That earned him a long, lingering kiss, complete with a little fingernail running across his back.

When I finally stopped, his low sound of satisfaction lingered in my ears.

"What's your story?" I asked him. "I mean, you're telling me I'm perfect, but the other night..."

"Oh, God. Cat. I'm really sorry about that. I mean, I'm not sorry, but..."

My brow furrowed and my eyes narrowed. "What?"

"Okay. So you know how I was at USC for the past two years?"

"Yeah."

"Well, I didn't tell you the whole reason why I left." His eyes darted away, focusing on his own hand as it moved over the sheet and rested on my hip. "When I was there...I didn't like myself very much. I did that bodybuilding thing I told you about, which is why I actually feel a little self-conscious right now."

"Okay, I don't believe that."

"It's true. I used to be in a lot better shape than this. But anyway, I got involved in some stuff I wasn't proud of. Some of it was really bad. And some of it was just sort of bad."

"Like?"

He sighed. "Oh, just....partying, I guess. I didn't party a lot, which is why when I did party, I partied hard. And I ended up in bed with too many girls that I didn't remember getting there with, you know?"

My eyes flew open and my eyebrows pushed up.

"No, no," he said. "No. I'm clean. Tested and everything. I swear. But the last time...I mean, I didn't even remember meeting the girl, you know? And it was just the worst feeling."

"Okay," I murmured, tracing his pecs with my finger. "So? What does that have to do with me?"

"God, Cat, that night I met you was just overwhelming. You were so gorgeous, I could barely think straight. And then realizing who you were... I mean, I've never forgotten what you did for me at Camp Eagle."

I giggled. "Little-kid egos, for the win."

"No, but really. The teasing could have gotten really bad, could have really fucked me up. You saved me that summer. I kissed the hottest girl at camp, and it got me major street cred."

I gave a closed-lip laugh and nestled my head into his shoulder. Jesus, the smell of his aftershave was enough to make me want to jump on him again right then and there.

"And your face, it's more gorgeous now, obviously, but really just the same. You've always been the perfect woman, to me. "

"Oh, stop," I said, kissing his neck. But I didn't want him to stop.

"So, only realizing who you were after I saw you in that class and wanted to lick every inch of you, and then the beer, and the dancing, and....well, to make a long story short, I didn't know which way was up, you know? And you'd been crying after the class, and you'd had some beer too."

"So?"

"So I made myself a promise a long time ago that I would never sleep with a girl unless I'd seen her at least twice. Not unless I woke up the next morning and couldn't stop thinking about her."

"You called me first thing the next morning."

"Pretty much. The first chance I got, or gave myself, anyway. So now you know. I couldn't stop thinking about you yesterday, and I don't think I'll be able to for a long, long time."

I grabbed his face and kissed with long and lingering kisses, biting at his lips and then stroking them with my tongue. I grinned when I felt his growing pressure against my stomach.

He dipped down, his mouth an unstoppable force against my skin. When he started kissing the slow path around my breasts again, I was a goner.

"I know that some people might consider this coercion," he whispered, "but at this point I kind of don't care."

Whatever he was going to ask me, I knew the answer would be yes. I could only get out a half-whimper, half-groan, and arched my back into his kisses.

"Would you please stay the night? I want to remember every second of this one, and I want every second to be with you."

I was absolutely right. "No" was never an option. I reached over to the nightstand, ripped open another square packet, and pulled the covers over the both of us, even though I knew they wouldn't stay there for long.

Chapter 11

As the weeks rolled on, I realized that I'd never had a real boyfriend before.

That probably sounded stupid, but it was true. I'd had fuck buddies. I'd had guys I was talking to, and who would take me out for dinner or dancing at nice places. And, since I'd been with Nate, I realized they were probably doing it for themselves.

Just like Jake, I realized all those guys had dropped off the map since I'd gotten back to Philly. And just like all the designers I'd worked with before my accident, they wanted nothing to do with me once I came back sixty pounds heavier.

The thing about Nate was, he made me want to tell all of them to fuck off. With Nate, I did two things I never had done that much of before the accident: Eat, and exercise. And I realized how much I loved to do both. In two weeks, we'd eaten the city's best sushi, Indian, Mexican, even Ethiopian. Nate knew all about food, and wine too, and he taught me how to appreciate the nuanced tastes of each dish and vintage.

One warm fall afternoon, wandering through the Reading Terminal Market with the sunshine streaming through the high glass windows and our fingers threaded together, Nate pointed out his favorite discoveries. "There are homemade pierogies and kielbasa, or the grape leaves at that place are to die for. And you're not leaving here without some Bassett's ice cream. Their Irish coffee flavor is just...wow."

As we walked by the produce stand, the vibrant peppers and lush greens decorating table after table, Nate stopped in his tracks. He headed to the stand with the herbs and basically caressed a bunch of green leaves. "This is gorgeous," he said to the shopkeeper.

"Comes from a little farm up in Chadd's Ford," she said, smiling. "Would you like to try some?"

Nate folded a leaf into his mouth, and his eyes fluttered shut as he chewed and moaned.

I giggled. "Foodgasm?"

"Understatement," he said, "of the year." He picked up the crate holding the bunches of basil. "We'll take it all."

"What are we doing? I'm starving," I complained as he handed some bills to the checkout girl.

"Have you ever wondered why we haven't eaten Italian?"

"Um...we've only known each other two weeks?"

"No. Because I make the best pesto you'll ever taste."

"And you're going to show me?"

We paused in the middle of the market, letting the noise and the light and the colors and the smells wash over us. He squeezed my hand, pulled me into him, and kissed me, steady and strong and lingering.

I'd never felt happier, or more treasured, with a guy. Which made me finally feel semi-okay in this body.

"Yes. And then I'm going to show you some of my other tricks."

"I'm so glad you didn't make me beg."

"Well, the night is young."

He dropped my hand and pinched my ass with his free fingers. I squealed and kissed his cheek, and two hours later, I was swooning over pesto sauce, pretty sure Nate wouldn't give a second thought to the garlic breath that followed.

One month later, I sat on the worn couch in Doctor Albright's office, warm light streaming through the windows. It was a welcome change from the gray, rainy chill that had seemed to settle over all of Philadelphia in early November. I didn't know whether it was the sunlight or the antidepressants, or just the past three weeks with Nate, but I was practically bouncing on the sofa.

When she stepped in, a smile broke across her face. "How are you, Catherine? You look well."

"I feel good," I said. I seriously could not control my grin.

"Is the medication working out for you?" she asked, peering down over her glasses.

"Oh. Um, I think so. I don't feel super different, but the mood swings aren't as bad as they used to be. Pretty nonexistent, actually."

"Yes, you are actually glowing. Did the nude modeling give you some sense of empowerment back? Professor Astor said you sat for her but needed to leave in the middle, and haven't called her since."

"Oh, you talked to her?" Was she allowed to do that?

"Just in passing. I've recommended the treatment before and I like to keep anecdotal evidence for whether it's working. Exposure therapy is relatively common, but that particular mode isn't. We're lucky to be at a university, and have access to unique things like human form drawing classes."

"Well actually, she was right. I didn't finish. I did two poses, and at the end of the second, I thought one of the guys in the class was complaining about my body."

"I see. And?"

"And he caught me crying on my way out, told me it was a misunderstanding. His eraser was breaking through the paper. That was all it was."

"But then, you haven't been back?"

"No, because...well, that guy turned out to be pretty great." That grin crept back up over my face and I was sure Doctor Albright could see every steamy moment that had passed between Nate and me. So I figured, what the heck, and told her everything—how he took me rock climbing to make me feel strong, and all the ways he made me feel sexy, too.

Doctor Albright made some notes in a small black book. It was so tiny that I wondered if she had a separate one for each patient.

"So, can you tell me about a typical week for you right now?"

"Usually I have class in the morning, I'll do some studying while I wait for Nate to get out of his classes. Then we'll do dinner, usually in, but sometimes out with friends. I spend some nights at the studio and the rest with him, typically."

"Mmm. Can you tell me whether that's different from your life last year?"

"Oh, yeah, completely. I mean..." I met her gaze to find an "I told you so" face there. Oh. Oh. That's what this was. "It's just that I've changed since the accident, you know?"

"How? You're still the same major, and you're still in a sorority, right? Still have the same roommate?"

My brain froze. "Yeah. Yes, you're right. But—"

"So what's different? Has your attitude changed?"

"Well, yeah. That stuff's not important to me. You know, partying and sorority stuff and everything."

"Why not? What's changed?"

I wracked my brain. I knew what she was asking, and I didn't want it to be the answer. But I knew it was, and eventually, I gave up. "My body."

"That, but more importantly, how you think of it as affecting you being in the world. I'm so happy you've found this man who makes you feel beautiful when you're with him."

"But?"

"But I worry about you tying your self-worth into only that. And I want you to consider that it may only be when you're with him. When you go to sorority events, how do you feel?"

I thought about the first TG of the season, which Nate couldn't make it to but where I stood against the wall all night. Or all the way back to that first night we went out, and Jake staring disdainfully at my body—a memory I really didn't want to relive. "I haven't even been to the clubs or anything this year. Wearing heels is tough, and…" Tears pricked at my eyes for the first time in weeks. "I hate it. I feel like I don't fit in."

"You're a normal size, Catherine. Are there are other girls in your sorority who wear a size ten, or twelve, or fourteen? Or at the clubs you used to go to?"

"I....well, yeah. I'm sure there are." I thought for a minute, and was able to pull out three names from the class of girls I'd entered the sorority with. "Yes. But..."

"But what?" Doctor Albright wore a small, sad smile, one that told me she knew she'd caught me.

"But they've always been that way?"

"I'm sure that's not true. They may have developed into their comfortable weight in seventh grade or in high school, or even in their freshman year of college. But they've learned to deal with it. You haven't, yet. And hiding behind Nate and how he makes you feel won't help you deal with it all the way. That's why I want to push you, Catherine. I do think we succeeded in nipping body dysmorphia in the bud. I really do. But now I want you to live with who you are. Right now. Yes, you have a boy to tell you you're beautiful, and when you're with him, you believe it. That is amazing. But now I want you to step outside that comfort zone. Push yourself. Find that feeling in yourself, instead of getting it from others."

A familiar pain, made up of a tight chest, a spiraling feeling in my head, and a lump in my throat, took over my whole body. I tried to hide it, I did. But there was no way. "Can't I just...I don't know. Make that my project next semester, or something?"

Doctor Albright leaned forward and covered my hands with one of hers. "I promise you, I'm telling you this for your own good. But you and this boy are young. So many things can happen, and his presence in your life is not guaranteed forever. I don't want him to become a crutch. Do you understand?"

I did. But I didn't want to.

I smiled a sad smile. "Okay. So, more exposure therapy?"

She mirrored my expression, and sat back. "Yes. Once a week, do something you used to do. Without Nate. Shopping with your friends—especially your very thin ones. A sorority event.Going out to a club.Maybe even modeling again."

"No, no. No. I can't model."

"Maybe we'll talk about that the next time. I'm actually thinking there's someone I could call."

Next time. She wanted to see me again. And she'd want me to model. Wasn't going to happen. Even though we still had half an hour in our session, I felt pricking behind my eyes. I got to my feet. I didn't want to cry in front of her.

"Thanks. I have to go."

I had my hand on the door when Doctor Albright called, "Cat. I know it's hard, but promise me you'll try. Or at least think about it."

I looked back over my shoulder, just out of the corner of my eye. "I promise." I wasn't sure I could do any such thing, but I just wanted to get the hell out of there.

The only thing that kept me from crying on the four-block walk home was the promise of tortellini with Nate's perfect pesto sauce that night.

Chapter 12

In the next week and a half, I did nothing to complete Doctor Albright's assignment. Whenever the idea popped up in my head, I was on the elliptical, or in bed with Nate, or teasing him through a recipe in his kitchen. I felt good. Why did I need to be in the real world? If spending all my time with Nate was what I needed to do to get through this semester, that was what I was going to do.

Yeah, Doctor Albright had been in my position. Sort of. The difference was that her weight hadn't been her entire identity, the one thing people thought of when they saw her. She hadn't been dumped based solely on her body, like I was.

Not that I even cared about asshole Jake anymore.

But because of Nate, at least I spent more time in the design studio than I ever had before. Any time I told him I felt huge, or ridiculous, he reminded me that it had to be either my attitude or my clothes. He could remind me that any of my body-image freakouts were unwarranted with a few strategically placed kisses. If it was my clothes making me feel horrible, we could figure out other options.

I'd learned the basics of sewing in my freshman and sophomore years, of course. But now I really got into it, learning how to turn a seam and make interesting structures for a model's body out of fabric.

I stood at one of the computers in Temple's fashion design studio surrounded by bolts of fabric and mannequins. All the mannequins were size fours, bigger than the average fashion model, weirdly, but still four full sizes smaller than me.

Nate strolled around the studio, stopping to gaze out the long windowed wall that looked out over the city. "God, the architecture just kills me. Can we come here some time at night? I want to see it lit up from this window. Drexel might not have a lot of things, but it does have an incredible view."

"Shut up," I said, through pins stuck between my teeth. I was pinning a heavy brocade to the mannequin for a waist ruffle on a dress that had a faux-wrap top. I'd had this idea in my head for weeks, but couldn't seem to get it right. It didn't help that my semester portfolio project, a collection that I'd have to present on the design school's catwalk in December, was looming.

"Very old-school," Nate said, walking over and assessing the design. "Very film noir."

My cell phone dinged in the pocket of my jacket, and through the pins jutting out of my mouth, I mumbled, "Can you get that? Joey might be texting me."

"We going out?" he asked, a tone of mild interest in his voice. He pulled the phone out of my coat pocket and swiped at it to read Joey's message.

"It's not Joey," he said. "E-mail from Doctor Albright? Your doctor e-mailsyou?"

I hadn't told Nate about Doctor Albright, for a couple of reasons. First, I was doing just fine. Second, I didn't want him to think his girlfriend—or whatever I was, since we hadn't talked about it—was a nutjob.

I dove for the phone, dropping the pins and letting them join the dozens of others that students had dropped on the floor. I clicked open the e-mail, and it looked like Doctor Albright had followed through on her promise to call someone for me. The e-mail said, *ANNOUNCING THE REAL WOMAN PROJECT – Competition to create eight original, inventive designs for America's real woman, sizes 12-16.* It went on to describe the event as a possible alternative to the end-of-semester portfolio project, and winning the highest votes from a panel of judges came with a five-thousand-dollar prize.

"This could be really great," I said, looking up at Nate and telling him the whole thing when he seemed interested. But as I read, his face fell.

"There was one of those back when I was at USC. Those poor fashion design majors." He shoved his hands into the pockets of his jeans.

"What? What happened?" I quirked an eyebrow.

"Well, they just…no one really took them seriously, you could say." He shrugged and walked away to pace in front of the huge glass windowed wall again.

"Nate? You okay?"

He still didn't meet my eyes. "Yeah. I just hate to think of you working so hard, and someone slamming you. You know?"

Was he just trying to protect me? He probably wasn't wrong—no one knew better than I did that my self-esteem was still pretty damn fragile. But five thousand dollars….I could pay for most of a semester with that. Especially without the extra hundreds I used to pick up walking runway shows here and there, and how much I was struggling this year, five thousand was a hell of a lot. I chewed on my lip. Something about his anxiousness was bugging me, something I couldn't put my finger on.

"But honestly," I placed my hands around the mannequin's waist. "Who is even this size? She would slip through your hands, or you would break her."

"You're right," he said, sounding more like his normal self. "Is there anything we can do to get a mannequin in here who's the size of an actual person? That a guy would actually want to sleep with?"

I rolled my eyes at him and picked up a new handful of pins. They slid cleanly through the fabric one by one as I smiled at the sheer satisfaction of being back in the studio again. At Nate being there with me. "According to the fashion magazines, you're one of the dumbest guys on the planet for wanting to sleep with a girl who looks like me. Not that I wouldn't want to be thinner."

"Seriously, though, what size are you?"

"I keep telling you," I laughed. "Twelve. Sometimes fourteen."

"And is that considered plus-sized, or whatever?"

I tilted my head and gazed at the mannequin. "It's a plus for you, because you're the only guy who wants to sleep with me."

"Nuh-uh," he leaned down and murmured in my ear. "Everyone wants to sleep with you. I see the way guys look at you."

"Oh," I said, turning in his arms and kissing him softly. "Then why am I bothering with you?"

A cocky grin spread across his face. "Because I take care of you.In more ways than one. And I'm sexy."

I giggled as my head fell back. "You do. And you are. But cut it out, because we don't know who else is going to walk in in the middle of the day."

"Oh, just give me a minute with your shoulder. You know how I love your shoulder."

A sigh escaped my throat as I brought my head forward again, exposing the area for him. "Remember when you told me that that was like a frame?"

"I never forget. I think of it every time I see you."

Which was a lot. He "saw" me almost every day. I was staying over at his place more than I was staying in the sorority house.

He kissed my shoulder, biting it softly, and pulled away. "Okay, I seriously do need to stop." He winced and grunted as he took a seat on one of the studio stools, adjusting the crotch of his jeans, and I grinned in satisfaction.

"That's what happens when you fool around in the studio."

"All right, well, I'll just have to help you out so that we can get home sooner."

His use of the word *home* with regard to the space we shared so often felt so good, so familiar, that I had to scold myself before I felt too good about it. Nate and I had been together only four weeks. We said a lot of things when we were in the middle of sex, and I'd almost screamed that I loved him in the middle of an orgasm, which he had become masterful at delivering to me.

But I always bit it back.For one thing, because it had only been four weeks, and for another, because I knew Nate, I respected his story, and I knew that "I love you" had to be based on something other than his incredible in-bed abilities and in-bed equipment.

Although I thought "I love you" to his chest every time he pulled off his shirt, I wouldn't tell him that.

"So, can you tell me about that design? The wrap top and cinching at the waist, what's that for?"

I stood back and cocked my head again. "I think it's just that those are the two parts of my body I really love. So I want to emphasize them."

"Yeah, but if you really look at what you're doing, it's a really sound architectural design. It's all about balance, you know? It's a matter of proportions. One thing balances out another. Damn, Cat. You know, we really are in the same career."

I beamed at him. "Okay, so can you tell me where the trouble is with this design, then? I can't figure it out."

He stepped back even further. "The bottom of the skirt."

"What's wrong with it?" I'd designed an A-line that skimmed over my saddlebags and ended just past my knees, so those thighs I hated so much would be completely covered.

"First of all, it's too long."

"You know I hate my thighs."

"And you know I'm obsessed with them," he said, his eye sweeping down over the yoga pants I'd taken to wearing with everything, probably in no small part because he said they looked good, and noticed how the seams lay kind of like riding pants. "But that's not the point," he said. "The balance is all off. You're tall enough that if you showed enough leg, it would put the legs that are exposed in a near perfect two-thirds balance with the rest of the dress. Even if you're not wearing heels...."

"Oh, I'm wearing this?"

"You can make it for yourself, right?"

"If I am, I will be wearing heels."

"You won't. It kills your shin, and when I rub your legs I want it to be sexy, not because you're in pain. There's no reason for you ever to be in pain."

"Except when you're kicking my ass at the rock wall, you mean."

"Yeah, but that's the good kind of pain. And at the rate we're going, you'll be kicking my ass by Christmas.

"Good kind of pain, indeed. It's the reason my arms will still look good in this dress."

"They'll look better out of it." He winked. "And the whole damn thing will look better if you bring the bottom of that skirt in."

"Are you kidding me?"

"No way." He bent down and pulled the skirt tight from the back. "See? Wide, gorgeous shoulders. Tucked-in waist. Round, incredible hips, shapely knees. They're all parts of a balanced whole. When two things are wide in a row, it doesn't look quite right."

Damned if he wasn't right. I smirked, raised my eyebrows, held the skirt right where his hands were, and slipped in a thick pin. We both stood back, assessing it. He let out a low wolf whistle, crossing his arms. "Great. Now just get a mannequin that's approaching your level of hotness and we'll have something to look at."

I spun around, grabbed his shirt, and kissed him hard on the mouth. "I'll give you something to look at," I said. "Your place or mine?"

"Your place," he said, "But not for what you're thinking. We're going out with Joey and a bunch of your friends. I asked her. I want us to do something you used to do. I want to get to know your friends. And you haven't been going out like you used to, you know?"

Great. Exactly the same thing Doctor Albright had said. It didn't matter whether he was suggesting it, or she was—I still didn't feel ready.

I pouted, but tried to make it look sexy. From the look on his face, it wasn't working.

He pulled me to him again. "You okay?"

I didn't quite feel okay, but I couldn't put my finger on why. "Perfect. Help me come up with something to wear?"

***

Two hours later, I stood in front of the mirror at my place, staring at every last one of my curves poured into a sequined black shift dress with a low neck and a mid-thigh skirt. "Your arms are fucking incredible, Cat. And that ass." He grabbed it, then spread his hands out over my stomach, bending in to kiss my neck.

"Okay, okay," I smiled. "Hands off, if we're going to make it out."

The club was not anything I would have chosen to go to—at least, not since my accident. My entire perception of college life had changed since then. Before, it had been about pushing my body to the limit—how little could I eat that day to look good in that dress, how crazily could I dance, how much could I party? Now, it was...well, I didn't know exactly what it was. But I knew I liked eating like a normal person, and I liked being with Nate. I liked tasting my food, and I liked savoring my time with him. I definitely loved how he made me feel. When it came down to it, I just really wanted to spend all my free time with him.

The very thing Doctor Albright was against.

I had pretty much stopped drinking since I met him, too. One, because he didn't party, and two, because I wanted to be fully conscious for every moment with him. Because of the abs, and also the incredible way he took his time with me, like I was just as important as school or family or anything else.

We caught a cab and had it take us to the edge of Old City Philadelphia. "Hayley said they'd been dying to try out this place since you guys got back. Awesome atmosphere, good dance music while still being relaxed. A place to rest your leg. There's no reason you should miss out on the Philly fun just because you have a stupid rod in there. "

I had texted with Joey, who had promised she was going to be there too, with anyone she could drag along. She was into indie music, and Robot Clive, a new techno group whose stuff had been making the rounds online, would be there. She was dying to hear them and so I believed she'd drag as many of our sisters as possible along with her.

When we pulled up to the bar, Joey and four of our sisters were waiting outside, fidgeting in the cold. "Oh, thank God," Joey gasped, tripping up to the cab and grabbing my arm to drag me closer to the girls. "It looks crazy weird in there and I didn't want to go in without you. Also, group discount."

Even though she was tiny next to me—I swore it felt like half my size tonight—Joey linked her arm in mine and tugged me inside. I wanted to wait for Nate, but the girls were already halfway through the door. Joey threw a glance over her shoulder. "Hey, Nate," she said. "You coming?"

Nate flicked his chin up, in a gesture that told me to go on ahead. It felt weird, but also natural, to be doing things with these girls again.

Inside, Fluid was one of the craziest and most eclectic places I had ever been. Short sets of stairs wound their way from the lower to upper levels and back again. One wall was covered in luxurious pillowed fabric, and the rest were given a mottled stone treatment. Arches sat at the top of every doorway, and curved metal banisters decorated the stairs. And the whole thing was bathed in a light, yet rich, blue light.

"It's like some creepy Hobbit lair," one of the girls said, and I joined in laughing. But seriously, holy shit, it was.

The light wasn't the only thing that glowed in the room. All the drinks in peoples' hands glowed starkly. "The alcoholic ones light up," Joey said. "It's like, a thing."

Nate sidled up to me and slid his hand around my waist, squeezing me right under my ribs. Right where I liked it. "What about the neon liquid?" he asked, leaning down to kiss my forehead.

"Oh, it's the alcohol," I said, making a face. I knew he was fine going out, but making it so obvious who was drinking and who wasn't seemed a little weird. I pushed up on tiptoes to whisper in his ear. "Is this okay?"

"Yeah, I'm fine. It's really not a big deal. I'm just not having one. Which kind can I get you?"

I twisted up my face, pushing an eyebrow down. I didn't want to make him feel weird, but there was no way I was getting out on the dance floor with all those slim, confident girls without a little liquid courage.

"Sweetie," he said, pulling my lips to his and kissing me slowly, "it's fine. What do you want?"

"Something sweet," I said, smiling gratefully.

Joey tugged on my hand, leading me toward a cluster of tables. "Come on, we're over here. Follow the glow," she said, winking.

A cluster of glowing pink and blue drinks led me right to Hannah, who was stroking hands and making out with Jake. The Jake.

Guess they'd gotten back together.

Panic fluttered through my chest and dropped into my stomach. Why didn't I think about the distinct possibility that Jake would be here? I'd scarcely thought of him since my first time with Nate, but now that I saw him it all came rushing back. The pretty decent sex we used to have. The way he laughed, throwing his head back and letting his Adam's apple bounce.

The way he smelled, like expensive cologne. Like someone the old me should have been in love with.

But, now that I'd been with Nate for just over a month, and seen how he'd taken an interest in me, not just sleeping with me—how he knew everything about me, and cared about my interests—the old me had never really been in love with Jake.

Especially after the way he had taken one look at me, after the most devastating event of my life as I knew it, and dumped me like a bad habit. Asshole.

Not that I missed him. At all. Still.

Game face.Game face.Game face. Hannah and Nate are friends. Maybe it would be fine if I kept the two of them between me and Jake. Then, Nate was behind me, brushing my hair to the side and kissing the back of my neck.

Hannah barreled out of her seat, launching herself at Nate and slinging her arms around his neck. He circled one arm around her waist and kept the other hand on me, so I wasn't jealous of her hugging him so much as I was jealous of how cute and petite her figure looked pressed up against his. It was like I'd always thought couples should look, with one beautifully muscled guy and one tiny girl.

Jake had never been beautifully muscled, and I had never been tiny. And we had never really been a couple, either, but seeing Hannah hugging Nate suddenly made me feel more self-conscious than I had in weeks. I gritted my teeth at the thought. I hated that I was slipping back so easily into thinking like that. Hated that as soon as I was with other people all I could do was compare myself to them.

I scooted into the next half-circle booth, sliding my suddenly huge-feeling ass against the smooth plastic all the way to the center, hopefully lessening my chances of having to ever get up. My hands wrapped around my drink and I stared at the pink glow between my fingers as I tried to focus on my breathing, and the fact that Nate had just kissed my neck, and his hand had barely left my body and how, right now, it was sliding over my knee. And how big he was, and how incredible, and how he wanted me. Not a tiny girl.

Joey ordered platters of appetizers—tiny gourmet pizza bites and miniature hamburgers.

I'd been crazy about food since I'd met Nate—not pigging out, but tasting it, enjoying it, learning what made me feel good and strong, and what made me feel like shit. But my stomach turned when I saw all this. Something was just...off. I couldn't picture putting food in my mouth.

It was only when I took a drink that I realized I probably should eat something, if only to absorb the alcohol. Between not having eaten dinner and not having drunk very much for almost a year, every one of my senses was already starting to feel fuzzy. The benefit to that was that the freaky insides of the club actually started to look kind of beautiful. Slowly, the food disappeared from the table, and slowly, the drinks were refilled. By the time I'd gone halfway through my second, I felt warm. Good. Relaxed. A little more alive than I had half an hour before. I talked with my friends, but I'd never remember what I was talking about. Something about recruitment next semester and training for a marathon—something I couldn't ever do—and some new show on TV. Everything was kind of a daze—a secure, warm one, though because Nate was right next to me, his hand on my thigh, talking to my friends. Like this was normal. Like this could be okay.

Doctor Albright was right there in my head again. "Do you feel okay without Nate? Or is he just a crutch?" Sure, it was nice to have him there, but this was okay. This was good. I felt fine. Or I did, until the girls started dancing. As always, most of them were at least half a head shorter than me.

They were all also just a little more than half my size, and watching their tiny bodies writhing in time to the music, clothed only in spandex stretchy dresses and skinny jeans on top of stiletto heels and tight tank tops. Everyone had arrived with jackets or cardigans, but it was so hot in this club that our booth was stuffed full with them.

Suddenly, I felt pretty hot too. I shrugged out of my coat and watched the sequins dance on the neck of my dress. It was so pretty when it swung under these lights.

It may have had something to do with the fact that Jake had left the booth about ten minutes earlier, doing God knows what, and now came back to the booth, holding out a hand for Hannah and pulling her to the dance floor. The techno had slowed to something much different, with a languid rhythm and pounding bass, from the throb that made drinking one and a half of those glowyconcoctions into something I was happy about instead of something I was starting to regret.

I looked down at my dress again. The bulge of my belly when I sat made it bunch up in a weird way and I just wanted it to stand up, stretch, even if I did tower over half the people there and reach the same height as most of the others.

I leaned over to whisper into Nate's ear, and oh Lord, when my lips brushed his neck it was so soft and warm and he smelled so Nate, that before I could even get any words out, I captured his earlobe between my teeth and ran my tongue along the underside of it. "Dance with me," I murmured, my hot breath blowing the musky scent of his cologne back at me. Delicious. I grazed his neck with my teeth, and he let forth a little moan followed by half a laugh.

"Jesus Christ," he said. "Why did I think it as a good idea to spend an evening with you out of the house?"

"That's what I said before," I murmured, drawing back and blinking some doe eyes at him. "But now we're here and I feel good. And I want to dance. And there's no way you're going home with anyone but me." His face twisted into a look of displeasure, but the music was too loud and I was too restless to stop and figure out what the hell was going on with him. We were here, and I was in a tiny, gorgeous dress, and the drinks were good, and my head was just a little fuzzy.

We got to the middle of a crowd of our friends and faced each other, linking our fingers together and slow dancing with my hips grinding against his. We were so close I could feel how stiff he was, even through the thick sequined fabric of my dress and his pants and boxers. I was about to reach for him in my fuzzy haze, but had to remind myself this was not the time or the place.

Nate let his hands clutch at my lower back, bunching up the fabric there and making it hike up my ass a little bit. I knew I was tall, but compared to him, I felt powerful, feminine. I'd even worn heels.

A round tray floated by with glowing blue shot glasses, and I took two. "Cat, I'm not…"

"No, I know. They're both for me," I said, as I threw down the first, then the second, leaning back to perch them on a nearby booth. My throat burned and my head whirled, but it was such a warm, soft feeling, like everything was beautiful. I'd missed it, I realized. I'd missed being out and drinking and feeling like I was relaxed and celebrating life. But I mentally stuck my tongue out at Doctor Albright. Nate was right here, and I was feeling this way. I turned around, and let him dance behind me, his hands resting on my hips. I leaned my head back against his shoulder, and he clutched me harder.

The beat picked up, the pounding music shaking the fixtures on the walls of Fluid. I turned around to face Nate again, and his hands pushed up through my hair. He covered my lips with his, tasting, playing with my tongue, and driving me absolutely fucking wild. When he sucked my tongue into his mouth, I moaned and pushed my fingers up underneath his shirt, splaying my fingers against his back."

"Hey, gorgeous. Hey." Nate chuckled in my ear. "No sex on the dance floor."

I whimpered as my hand brushed down the front of his pants. "No one would notice," I murmured. "I'm...substantial."

"You are absolutely beautiful. But no. They would notice. I'm just as tall as you are."

My tongue was thick and soft in my mouth. One more shot, and I wouldn't be able to feel my lips. Here, in the middle of the dance floor, with everything wavering and my arms clinging to Nate, I felt okay. As long as I didn't look at the other girls, how skinny they were. I hated that I was comparing myself to them, but I told myself that I had to remember I had always done that, even before I'd gained all this weight.

"I have an idea. Let me walk you to the ladies' room, I'll go get our coats from the coat check, and meet you back there. And then we'll get you home."

"And into bed?"

"Yes, I will pull off this dress and we will go to bed." God, his voice was sexy. Why had I never noticed how sexy his voice was before?

I turned my head back and kissed him, long and slow, then pulled back and gazed at him from beneath heavy, half-closed eyelids. The music pounded around us, and the streams of colored light cutting through the blue glow that lit up the room felt like bars of a cage. Suddenly, the warm buzz was wearing off, and I felt how cold the club was as I left the crowd of dancers and crossed my arms in front of me, loving the bounce of my boobs but hating the jiggle of my thighs as I made it to the ladies' room. I used the toilet, then stood at the sink and stared at myself in the mirror.

The fuzziness had almost completely left and been replaced by the cold fluorescent light of the concrete-walled restroom and the hideous image of my own smudged lipstick and makeup. Not to mention my hair frizzing at the surface and sticking to my forehead, making me look like I'd half fallen into a puddle.

I was an absolute disaster. How much had I drunk?

I straightened up, wiping my lipstick back into place as much as possible and evening my foundation out with a paper towel moistened under the faucet. At least I'd been smart enough to wear waterproof mascara, which always stayed on for more hours than I would have actually liked.

I smoothed down my hair, too, wetting my hands and running my fingers back through it. It would freeze outside, but we were going home. Out of the bathroom and into the swirling lights and bodies of the club, I made my way along the wall, circling the large dance floor in the middle. I didn't want to get caught up in it and be stuck there in the club, among those girls that made me look so humungous and clumsy-drunk. Head to the front coat check and find Nate and get home as quickly as possible. I wrapped my arms around my waist, suddenly self-conscious. I didn't belong back out here, and I didn't know why Doctor Albright—or I—ever thought I did.

Small hallways shot off of the main room at odd angles, and as I passed one, someone's hand darted out and grabbed my wrist. I tripped over my own shoe, trying to stay upright in the dark, narrow passageway. My hand hit the wall, and my body pressed up against someone.

In the split second it took for my eyes to adjust to the dark with blue tinge from the dance floor, I thought it might have been Nate. But I knew it wasn't.

A pair of eyes, level with mine, stared hungrily into mine. "Jake," I breathed. I stood up straight, removing my hand from the wall, and ripped my wrist from his hand. It didn't deter him for a second. He reached out, grabbed my ass, and pulled me tight to him. I could practically feel his raging hard-on push between my legs, and I wanted to vomit.

"Goddammit, Jake," I yelled, twisting myself out of his arms. "I'm not sleeping with your sorry ass. I wish I hadn't, ever. And even when I was, I wouldn't have done so in this skeezy hallway." I smoothed down the front of my dress, muttering, "Last time I saw you, you wanted nothing to do with me, and now you try to grab me in the dark nightclub hallway?"

"Yeah, well, last time I saw you, you looked miserable, but tonight you looked good. Nice tits. Just drunk enough for a fast fuck, with handles for grabbing."

Jake reached out and pinched my side, and my skin crawled. I spun around and slapped him as hard as I could across the face. Then I rolled my eyes and turned to walk back out to the dance floor. "Next time you grab some girl, maybe don't do it with your fucking girlfriend in the other room." I took two more steps, and then Jake's hands dug into my waist, then one moved up, squeezing my boob. Then a slimy tongue shot into my ear.

I was acting on pure instinct. I pulled my fist in toward my stomach, then whirled around my left shoulder, elbowing him in the stomach. One of his hands dropped, but the other held on. With a grunt, I raised my heel up and brought it down on his toes.

"Motherfucker!" he screamed.

"Just be grateful my boyfriend didn't let me wear stilettos, you skeezebucket. And be grateful he didn't see this, or that pretty face of yours would be unrecognizable right now."

The buzz of the alcohol was definitely gone now, replaced by a killer headache digging into my temples and making my limbs shudder. All I wanted was to get the hell out of there. I stalked back out onto the dance floor, plowing straight through the crowd this time.

Nate found me, caught my hand in his, raised it to his lips and kissed it.

"Sweetheart, you're shaking. You okay?"

"No. I mean, yeah. Now I am."

He drew back from me, examining my face, smoothing my hair back from my face. My God. I must have been a disaster. "Just that guy, the one who snubbed me?"

"He's here?"

"Yeah, he's actually Hannah's boyfriend."

A mix of surprise and alarm took over his face. "Why didn't you tell me? We were sitting at the same table as the fucker."

"I didn't think it was important. Because it's not. Anyway, he tried to…talk to me. Just now."

"Don't tell me he tried to touch you."

"He did, but it's no big deal." I wouldn't let it be. I wouldn't let that asshole get to me again.

A storm brewed behind Nate's eyes, and before I could convince him otherwise, he was stalking back across the dance floor. Jake was still recovering, leaning against a wall. In one smooth motion, Nate had pulled Jake upright by the collar of his t-shirt, and spoke in a low growl just inches from his face.

"If you ever so much as think about talking to this woman again, trust me, I will sink to actually laying my hands on you, do you understand?"

No swearing. No yelling. No punching. But Nate succeeded in scaring the shit out of Jake, because when he let him drop, Jake raised his palms in front of his chest and stammered apologies.

"Come on, sweetheart," he said, grabbing my hand, and circling his other arm around my waist as he walked me back out.

"You didn't have to do that."

He looked up at me with round eyes.

"But I appreciated it."

Even though I could take care of resident assholes all on my own, I loved that Nate had stood up for me. I also loved that he didn't cause a scene, because I didn't want that—not right now, not even over me. In fact, the only thing I did want was to get home with him, wash my face, strip off all my clothes, slide under the covers, and be content knowing that me—exactly as I was, only me—was exactly what Nate wanted.

Fuck what Doctor Albright had said. I wasn't my old self, and I wasn't going to be. If I was happy being with Nate, I was just going to keep being with Nate. Even if he was a little bit of a crutch, it wasn't like he didn't know anything about my past.

This was honest. This was good.

I told him as much, tucked my head into his shoulder while his hand went around my waist, and he nodded against my head.

We settled into a cab, which I guess he'd called when I went to the bathroom, and only broke that position to get our seatbelts on. I sat in the middle, letting my head bounce against his arm as we cruised through the neon-streaked city night.

We walked up to his apartment, and I stumbled to his bathroom, where I rinsed my mouth out, scrubbed my teeth, and rinsed my mouth out again. I scrubbed my makeup off and swiped a steaming washcloth over my eyes for good measure.

Nate was waiting to get into the bathroom on my way out. I walked up to him, then fell into him, letting my forehead rest against his chest. "Okay if we just go to bed?"

"Yeah, of course. You feeling okay?"

I wasn't feeling okay. I felt like I'd been hit by a truck and slithered over by a snake all in one night. But I didn't want to tell him that. "Just a headache."

"Sweetheart. Let me take care of you. You should have told me in the cab, I would have brought you Tylenol right away."

He tugged me over to the bed by my hand, reached behind me, and unzipped my dress. It fell to the floor. The thong I'd put on to make my ass flawless in that dress suddenly felt like a cage, so while Nate drew back the sheets I stepped out of that, balling it up and shoving it in my purse next to my side of the bed. I slid into bed, in all my naked glory, but Nate seemed less concerned with his girlfriend being naked in his bed and way more concerned about whether I would rather have Tylenol or Advil. He tucked the heavy covers around me as he asked the question, and was back with three extra-strength Tylenol when I told him.

The rush of the water from the bathroom as he got ready for bed was a blissful minute and a half of white noise. Part of me wanted to tell Nate about what Jake had done, and the loudest part of me screamed that he would never be doing that again, so what was the point? And besides, nothing had really happened.

Nate walked back into the room, standing next to the bed as he kicked off shoes and stepped out of his pants. Through the thin light and the pounding of my head, I watched those gorgeous shoulders shrug out of his button-down shirt, leaving an undershirt. Then he started to slide into bed next to me.

"No," I complained, "Take your shirt off. Please?"

He raised an eyebrow at me. "You have a headache." I knew he was saying I was drunk, and he didn't want to. But instead of going for begging, I went for teasing.

"Yeah, too bad you didn't catch me on the dance floor, right?"

"You know that's not why I—"

"No, I know. I'm just kidding." I stretched my naked arm up to him, and watched my muscles flex. Yeah, there it was. My beauty was back, when I was here with Nate. "But I do want you to take your shirt off. I want to feel you next to me. I swear, I'm falling asleep in like two minutes."

An indulgent smile stretched across his face. "You know I'd do anything for you."

I tried to look away as he pulled it over his neck, because the sight of those particular muscles doing that particular act had actually sent me into a frenzy the other day. But right now, I was exhausted, and I looked and smelled disgusting.

More than anything, I just needed him to hold me.

In seconds, his arms were around me, rocking me briefly away, then pulling me into him. In a few seconds more, his body felt heavier on my arm. "You're more exhausted than I am, huh?" I asked.

"It's been a long time since I went out dancing. I'm just glad you were there with me. Gave me something to focus on."

"Exactly the way I felt."

I snuggled my face into the warm, smooth skin of his chest, while his face pressed into my hair. "Jesus, your hair stinks."

I laughed, sinking down farther. "Oh, shit. Sorry. The cigarette smoke always gets caught in there."

"Stop that. Don't ever apologize for being you, and being here," he murmured, tugging me back up on his chest and drawing my lips to his. No intensity, no tongue. Just himand me, and this moment of perfection. For only me, just as I was, even if "as I was" was smelling like a gross club that I'd dragged him to even though he really, really really didn't want to go.

I felt my own body getting heavy, exhaustion taking over and pulling me deep into sleep. Nate was already breathing deeply, and right before I nodded off, all I could think about was how nothing could ever screw this up.

***

It was the deepest sleep I remembered ever having in my whole life, wrapped up there in Nate's arms, warm and accepted. By the time my eyes began to flutter open, there was enough light filtering in through the window that my lids lit up with a warm glow. Nate's arms went around my shoulders, and his lips grazed against my nose. I sighed, stretching my lips up to his. But when I slid my tongue along his bottom lip, there was an obviously minty taste to his breath.

I pulled away and he groaned. "Hey. What are you interrupting my kisses for?" His arms slid down and around my waist, pulling me close to him. He had thick sweatpants on, and I groaned.

"When did you brush your teeth? And more importantly, why did you put pants on? Why would you want to ruin my morning like that?"

He laughed, a chuckle low in his throat. "I made you breakfast."

"Does it come with a side of man candy?" I asked, running my hand down his back. Damn, the muscles just didn't stop.

"What did I do to deserve this objectification?" He cupped my face in his hand and tried to kiss me again, but I dipped my head down, pressing my lips against his neck again, then sliding lower. Oh, Jesus. There was that shoulder muscle. I just had to lick it. I reached up to wrap my arms around his neck, just to get more of myself against more of him.

When I did, the smell from my armpits smacked me in the face. I was rank, and now that I was completely sober, I was actually able to realize it.

My body stiffened, and Nate drew back. "What? Is this about the morning breath?"

"That, and the fact that I partied and drank last night and my armpits could kill you with too much exposure." He opened his mouth to protest, but I pushed out of the bed. "No way. I cannot do this unless I feel sexy too, remember?"

He rolled his eyes a little and fell back on the pillow, groaning. "Get out of here, then."

I froze as he rolled over, burying his face on the pillow. My heart completely stopped. No fucking way he was kicking me out for not having sex with him.

"Towels are under the sink. Your hair's gonna smell like guy."

I barely made out the words for how muffled they were against the pillow.

I sucked in a breath again. "Holy shit, Nate. I thought you were kicking me out."

He sat bolt upright. "What? This has something to do with seeing that asshole Jake last night, doesn't it? Cat, you have to know I would never—"

"No," I grumbled, tugging open his drawer and pulling an old t-shirt over my head. "Just forget I said anything." Overreact much? What was wrong with me?

I stood up, mostly covered, and traipsed to the bathroom, grabbing my toothbrush out of my purse, before he could say another word.

I flipped on the water, then stopped at the sink for thirty seconds to brush my teeth. Scour them, more like. After a few more seconds, I'd finally removed the scuzz from my teeth and bad breath from my tongue. I stepped into the shower

194

and sighed. The water pounded on my back, steaming up the entire room. I loved a hot shower almost as much as I loved ice cream or a huge fluffy sweatshirt—it was one of the indisputable pleasures of life. I could feel all the smoke and filth and fuzzy drunkenness washing off of my skin, and as I really thought about the difference between the two feelings—nasty versus clean—I wondered why I'd ever liked going out anyway. Maybe I'd never minded the nastiness of it because I'd never shared bed space with someone the morning after.

There was one bottle of combination hair and body wash in the shower, in a black and ice-blue bottle with an aggressive-looking font on it—guy stuff. I cursed myself for not bringing some of my own toiletries earlier. We'd only been together five weeks—and never talked about how "together" we were—but I stayed over all the time. I fumbled, wet and freezing in the cold air outside the shower, through the clutter under his sink, and somewhere between the toilet bowl cleaner and box of extra razor blades I found a couple of hotel bottles of shampoo and conditioner, and breathed a sigh of relief. At least he was wrong about that—my hair would not smell like boy.

I stepped in, and the water was a perfect scaldinghot on my skin. I sighed, and rolled my neck to the front, closing in my eyes and breathing in the steam.

Then I felt a small burst of cool air, and my neck snapped up. The door was open just a crack, and Nate's muffled voice floated into the bathroom, drowned out by the rushing water and blocked by steam.

I rolled my eyes and smiled, trying to ignore the pang in my heart and twist in my gut from what I thought he'd been telling me earlier. I thought I needed to get in the shower to get away from him. But as his unintelligible speech hit my ears, my heart calmed, and I felt better. Stronger.

"Come in here, crazy," I said, laughing.

The door opened even further, and I hugged my chest. "Hurry up, though. You're letting in all the cold air."

"I just wanted to see if you found everything you needed," Nate said as he stepped in, and even through the steam, the line of his shoulders was strong. Irresistible. And suddenly, all I wanted to do was grab him. All of him.

"Everything but one thing," I said, grabbing the sliding glass door and peeking out.

He turned his head over his shoulder, and I'd be damned if those weren't the sweetest puppy dog eyes I'd ever seen on anyone. "I'm sorry about...in there. I really didn't mean for you to think...shit, Cat. I'm sorry."

"No, it was me. I was being stupid." I was. Nate had never done a single thing to make me think that he wouldn't want me for not having sex with him. "It was my own stupid paranoia. You're perfect." He was.

Nate half-turned and leaned in to kiss me. Then he smiled, keeping his hands to himself. "Okay, well I'm going to continue to be perfect and finish making the breakfast I just started.

I darted my arm out of the shower and grabbed at the chest of his t-shirt. "Nuh-uh. Breakfast can wait. But I can't."

I'd known as soon as he'd walked in that this was not going to end without me dragging him into the shower too. I grinned as he leaned in for another kiss, but broke it just as quickly to pull the t-shirt up over his head. The bulge under his pajama pants was obvious, and quickly turning into a tent instead of a bump. He kissed me again, and my thumbs hooked into his pants, pulling him in and them down at the same time. In a second, he was in the shower, naked and muscled and all mine, standing at serious attention.

I giggled.

"What is so funny about this?" he murmured, pressing his hands into the small of my back and pulling me close to him. The sheer sensation of his hot, tight body pressing against mine and the steaming water flowing over us made me gasp into his mouth.

He moved his lips down my jaw and into the crook of my neck, his steaming breath sending shivers through my body. When he sucked on the tender skin at the base of my throat, my hands drifted down to his gorgeous ass, squeezing and pinching like I wanted to climb him. Because I did, desperately.

He pulled his mouth away from me, and I whimpered.

"This is very sexy, sweetheart, but are you sure this is okay? There aren't any covers, and the light's still on..."

"It's more than okay. I know you want me no matter how I look."

He kissed at my jaw, then pressed his lips to each of my cheeks, then each of my eyelids. Then his tongue licked into my mouth, slowly, languidly, running over every surface of my tongue and lips.

Jesus.

My hands slid over his back, and I dug my nails in as his hardness bobbed against the inside of my thigh. A burst of wanting warmth shot up between my legs. I had to have him. Now.

But then he rested his hands on my hips, pushing one and pulling the other, so that I turned around to face the water. In an instant, one of his arms wrapped around my stomach and the other reached for a mesh sponge and a bar of soap resting next to it.

"I've already washed ..." My voice sounded weak.

"I know." He sounded mischievous, and I liked it. "I just want to feel you up a little more."

I giggled, and arched my back so that my stomach pressed out against his splayed fingers, long and strong like always. Something about seeing them covered in soap and smoothing over the soft roundness of my belly made them about ten times sexier, and suddenly I only wanted them to be doing one thing.

Just like he read my mind, Nate slid his hand down between my legs, and started flicking and circling every sensitive spot he'd discovered in the last couple of weeks.

A feeling like warm honey shot up all over my body, and my knees felt weak. But I couldn't break his hold on me. Everything felt too good, including his other hand, which was now brushing the hair off my neck and kissing down my spine, then out toward my shoulder.

"I know last night was less than ideal, but my God, you were gorgeous on that dance floor. It was like a whole different, equally incredible you. Who was that Cat?" he asked, his tongue flicking against my collarbone.

He must have been talking about the pre "Busting-Jake-up" Cat.

I smiled, but I knew it wasn't a good one. Not my usual genuine one, so I turned and kissed him, moaning as his thumb rubbed against my most sensitive spot, and sucking on his tongue.

He grunted and spun me around again, kissing me even harder and tangling his fingers through the wet blonde waves at the back of my head.

But then he pulled back, fluttering gentle kisses up along my cheekbones, then kissing the tip of my nose. The growing hardness between my legs told me he was dying for more, but the expression on his face and the gentleness in his voice told me something else. "Seriously, though. You looked so happy out there until…you didn't anymore." I realized I'd never seen his eyelashes wet before. Somehow, the way they were darkened by the water droplets made the sparkle in his eyes even more pronounced.

"I don't know," I said. "For a second I felt like my old self. But it was probably the alcohol."

"What do you mean, your old self?" he asked, pressing a lingering kiss to my lips before looking into my eyes again.

"I don't know. Confident.Happy in a crowd."

"Why only for a minute?"

"Because, I'm not the same person I used to be. And as soon as the alcohol wore off a little bit, I was back to the me I am now. The only one you've ever known, I guess." I shrugged like it didn't matter. But I knew he could tell it did.

He caught my chin with two fingers, and held my gaze to his. "Well, I love the you I know now."

My heart beat wildly in my chest. Had he just told me he loved me? I didn't want to ask, and couldn't even if I did, because his mouth was back on mine, sweet and exploring and wanting. Patient and desperate all at once. One of his hands cradled my jaw and the other played at the nape of my neck, and for just that moment, with the pattering of water against the walls and the steam hiding everything but the curves of our bodies, I could imagine the world belonged entirely to us.

And then I knew, with all of me, that he did love me, and that I loved him too, and suddenly hearing it wasn't so important anymore. But having him even closer was.

From behind, his length slid against me, and even though everything was hot and wet, the heat of the two of us together was so sweet, and so incredible, that I wriggled against him even closer, dying to have him inside. He kissed and licked down my neck, sucking and biting as he went, while my hand circled him down below. Then, with a groan, his hands were on my breasts, his thumbs flicking at the now-hard beads at the front. Dipping his head, he sucked one deep into his mouth, drawing back after a few seconds and circling my nipple with his tongue, then tugging it between his teeth ever so gently before moving to the other side and giving it similar treatment.

Pleasure shot through me, and there was nothing but the steam and the water and stars swimming around my head at how absolutely incredible and treasured I felt in that moment.

But after another few seconds, it still wasn't enough. I didn't think it would ever be enough.

"I want you," I managed, my voice hushed and ragged.

Another low rumble from his chest, and he had me turned around again, and nudged me toward the back wall of the shower. One of my hands gripped the towel bar, and the other splayed out on the wall beside it. His hand covered mine, our fingers interlacing, while his breath breathed hot against my ear, driving me wild.

"Let me just grab a condom," he said. I swore if he left me, I would collapse in a quivering heap right there on the floor, so I turned and kissed him, biting his lower lip when I pulled back.

"Don't," I pleaded. "It's fine. I'm on the pill, and I trust you." I reached back and let my hand slip around him again. He groaned.

"Please," I said.

His forehead fell against my shoulder, and then, with one firm thrust, he was inside. Dear Lord, I had never felt anything so incredible in my life. There was something raw, something primal, something utterly trusting, about the white-hot skin-on-skin sensation of just him inside of me with nothing between us.

Not to mention that from this angle he was deeper than he'd ever been.

While one of his hands held mine against the wall, steadying me, the other caressed my most sensitive spot, driving me absolutely wild. His hot length plunged in again and again, urgent yet controlled, like he was thirsty and wanted to take long, slow, deep drinks of me for as long as he could stand it.

His fingers never left my clit, flicking and teasing at first, and then, as his rhythm inside became even stronger, deeper, more intense, rubbing in hard, steady circles.

I arched my back to let him even deeper inside, and his balls slapped against my ass, punctuating the urgency with which he drove into me. He sucked at the space just below my ear, and between that and the all-encompassing pleasure of his hand in front of me, I had no choice the mounting orgasm burst all the way through me, starting at my core and rippling through all my limbs.

My body clenched around him again and again as a long, low moan trembled out of my throat. A second later, his hand moved from between my legs to wrap all the way around my stomach and hold onto me as if for dear life. I hadn't thought he could get any harder, but as my body spasmed over his, he was like steel inside me, driving faster and faster in short, deep thrusts, until finally, his moans joined mine, echoing off the tiled shower walls.

We stood there, still joined together, for just a second until he pulled out. He turned me around again and devoured me with long, satisfied kisses balanced with knowing grins and panting from both of us.

"I think you need to hold me up," I said. "I'm all shaky."

"You and me both, sweetheart."

He reached for the mesh sponge again and ran his hand gently between my legs. "Let's get cleaned up a little bit, and then I want to feel every inch of you with my fingers. And my tongue."

"And maybe your teeth a little?" I whispered, craning my neck up just enough to capture one of his earlobes between mine.

He chuckled softly, and I felt him twitch against my thigh again.

"My, my. I'd say that's a yes."

I disentangled from him and stepped out of the shower, grabbing one of the guy-smelling towels hanging on the back of the door and pulling it tight around my chest.

"No. That's a hell yes." He reached under the towel and pinched my ass, and I squealed and ran out of the bathroom, tumbling into the bed. For once, I didn't care if the lights were on or my hair was wet or my makeup had gone. And when he jumped in after me, and kept his promise to explore every inch of me for the rest of the morning, I was pretty sure he didn't, either.

Chapter 13

We were three weeks from Thanksgiving break, and none of my e-mails had delivered a good deal on the flight I needed to get back home to California. By this time last year, my account had had a few extra thousand dollars in it from modeling gigs, and I'd barely blinked before dropping eight hundred of it on a ticket home to see my dad. Bouncing from house to house always sucked anyway, but there was something about those stolen moments lounging on the couch with my brother in our PJs that made it all worth it. I would have gone back to Ohio, but my mom was using the holiday as an excuse to party in Vegas with her best friends. Everything was cheaper over Thanksgiving, she'd said.

Finally, I found a flight that would get me home in time for Thanksgiving in the six-hundred-dollar range. I had barely more than that in my bank account.

I booked the flight, entered my debit card information, and was just daydreaming about the shopping trip I'd hopefully be able to get my stepmother to take me on and the new riding boots I'd been coveting, since my old ones had been beat up by the Philly streets, when the site refreshed with an angry red bar up top.

Something has gone wrong with your payment information. Please try a different card, or enter the information again.

My heart stopped. "What the hell?" I muttered as I navigated to my bank's website and hastily signed in. When the account page loaded, I felt sick to my stomach. My hand flew to my mouth and I shook my head. "Dammit," I said. "Dammit." The screen read, plain as day, *Account balance: $232.18*.

"What the hell?" I repeated as tears welled in my eyes. I couldn't ask my parents for more money—Mom didn't have any, and Dad had already cautioned against asking. I had to stay in a budget, he said. My brother was broke.

I didn't have a credit card. Dad had always taught us that we shouldn't have one, especially if we didn't have a guaranteed steady income, and I'd always had plenty of cash last year. I wasn't going to get one just to go home for Thanksgiving. It wasn't that big of a deal.

Except, when I thought about staying in that big house all by myself eating a sad frozen meal—and probably, let's face it, some raw cookie dough—a lump rose in my throat. That's when there was a soft knock at the door, and Nate's head popped in.

"Hey, sweetheart, Joey let me up. I brought you some coffee since we're staying up late studying, and—oh, shit. What's up?" He dropped his bag right inside my door and strode over to me in a few steps, setting the coffee down on my desk before kneeling down and looking me in the eye.

Now the tears were rolling, prompted by his concern.

"Nothing," I said. "It's nothing. I just…California flights are expensive, and I guess I spent more than I thought this semester already. That's it," I muttered, shuffling papers around on my desk.

"So just put it on a credit card. You'll figure it out later."

"I don't have one." I told him the whole story, and he nodded, watching me.

"Let me buy it, then. Thanksgiving present from me to you."

"There's no such thing as Thanksgiving presents," I laughed. I swiped the tears from under my eyes, checking quickly to make sure none of the waterproof mascara had flaked off.

He leaned in and kissed the corner of my mouth, whispering against my lips, "I know. But I just hate seeing you cry."

I laughed. "I'm okay. Really."

"You want to get back to Cali that much, huh?"

"Oh, it's not that, it just that …I don't know. All my roommates are going, and…oh, shit." I'd been so self-centered I was realizing it too late. He thought I was inviting myself home with him. That half-happy, half-mischievous look in his eye confirmed it. "No, no," I stammered. "You don't have to…"

"No, but you do. Have to come home with me for Thanksgiving. It's only two and a half hours north. We can come back that night," he said with a wink, and I laughed again.

"I really didn't mean to invite myself."

"My mom would kill me if she found out not only about the existence of you, but the fact that you were all alone back on campus on Thanksgiving, without me bringing you home with me."

He was already down on his knees so he could hug me as I sat in my desk chair, but now he took both my hands in one of his. And when he said my name, I swooned and wanted to jump him all at once. "Cat, formerly known as Hot Katie, will you please come home with me for Thanksgiving?"

I couldn't bring myself to say "yes." It was way too cheesy for this guy and this moment, and so I just leaned down, snaking my hands under his arms and pressing my lips to his, then whimpering as his tongue slid against my bottom lip. A few minutes later, we pulled apart, and he stood up, holding his hand down to me. I took it and stood next to him, leaning in for one more quick kiss. "Oh, she's gonna love you."

The few weeks between then and Thanksgiving passed in a blur. I worked my ass off for my portfolio, and managed to come up with a few decent designs. They weren't perfect, and I didn't have all eight designs I needed for the competition, but I reasoned that I'd tackle it after Thanksgiving. I'd always worked better under pressure, anyway, and maybe panic would be a good substitute for inspiration.

I never tried to go back out to the bar again. Even though the shower marginally fixed my mood, it had been so awful the night of, and I was working so much and studying the rest of the time that I couldn't bring myself to go out again. On top of that, Nate gave me not only a drawer at his house, but an entire dresser. A few weeks later, most of the clothes I owned that actually fit me lived there, and I was bringing groceries back to his place so he could cook me dinner while I sketched designs for new clothes.

More and more often, I knew my designs would look way better on a plus-sized girl.

I had to admit, a not-so-small part of me was pretty damn excited about going home with Nate. Every time I was with him, I felt like we connected on a new level. And even though the L-word hadn't been repeated since that one time in the shower, the way he listened to me talk, the way he took care of me, and the way he gave me such careful attention under the covers told me he loved me. I loved him too, without a doubt in my mind.

Doctor Albright's voice still popped into my head from time to time, but I reasoned that it had only been a couple of weeks since I'd seen her, and I'd taken care of step one. Or, at least, the step one I'd translated her "pose nude" assignment into—Get Naked In Front of a Guy.

I'd done that. Hell, I'd let him fuck me from behind in the shower. That had to count for triple points.

I sighed as I stuffed things into my backpack at Nate's house, just so I could take them home to stuff in my suitcase. I hadn't wanted to drag my empty suitcase to his house to fill it. I shoved panties and pajama pants into my backpack, and a stray sweatshirt of his I hoped he wouldn't notice was missing.

"Hey, thief." His warm voice rolled over my shoulder as his arms went around my waist. Over the last few weeks, I'd started to barely even notice when he touched a part of my body I was very sensitive about—it just didn't even matter. There came a time in every relationship when, if someone had kissed and licked and sucked every part of you enough times, you became pretty damn sure they liked your body. Even if you didn't.

Being there with Nate was amazing, to say the least.

"Keep stuffing that bag," he murmured into my ear. "We need to be on the road in an hour."

"Yeah?Really?" I had thought we had more time.

"Yeah."He stood up and running a hand through his hair. "Change of plans. Mom has a new boy toy she wants me to meet, and it was either dinner the night before Thanksgiving or Thanksgiving itself. And I swear, these guys are getting more and more ridiculous."

"So Thanksgiving dinner would be…."

"A bad idea. I think. I don't know. I don't have any sibs to make the buffer zone. And California is too far away to impulsively flee."

"It's too bad, you know," I said. "It might be kind of fun to go back to camp. Where we first met."

"Oh, my God. Why would you ever want to go back there?"

"I don't know. Nostalgia?"

"You might have had a great summer there, but all I remember outside of that one sweet kiss was being the fat kid everyone tortured." He shuddered. "No."

"Oh." I'd never thought of it that way before. The fact that the memory of camp hurt him hurt me, too. I nodded. "Okay, pick me up in a couple hours?" I asked, shouldering my backpack and heading for the door.

Nate caught my belt loop and pulled me back toward him, crushing his mouth to mine. "Sweetheart, please," he said, his voice husky. "Let me drive you back. I'm really not interested in letting you out of my sight for the next three days."

I giggled, pressing in again and letting my tongue sweep into his mouth. "That's just fine with me."

The drive up to Wilkes-Barre would have been boring, with its straight-as-an arrow turnpike road framed by endless flat farmland and gray sky, but, I realized as the car barreled north, we'd spent a lot of time together over the past six weeks. Even though the sex was great, and there was a lot of it, most of our time was spent just being together. Cooking, talking, laughing. We had so much in common, between our divorced parents and summers in California and the similar majors, that talking to him was easy. Like an extension of myself, or the new self I'd been since the accident.

"How's your leg feeling these days? Think you'd be up for a hike?" He stroked his thumb against the back of my hand. I hadn't even realized my other hand was gripping my shin, folded beneath me on the heated seat of the SUV he'd rented.

"It's been bugging me a little, but that's because I haven't been working out enough."

"Too much studio time?"

"Kind of." I had been pushing to get my portfolio built up, but that was all he knew. I hadn't told him about the contest, or about how his architecture-inspired insights had been so influential on my work. Mostly because I wanted it to be a surprise, and a little bit for some other reason I hadn't quite figured out yet. "So yes. I'd love for you to show me around. Show me everything else, too."

"Okay. I'm warning you right now. It's a hick town—like, a strip mall and a motel and a couple restaurants. Oh, and a casino."

"A casino? Fancy."

He threw his head back and laughed. "Hardly. Just a bunch of slot machines and a restaurant that serves mushy pasta and oily mozzarella sticks. And a Holiday Inn attached to it attempting to be fancy. Which, actually..." He dropped my hand to pick up his phone and scroll through the messages, read one, and groaned. "Yep. Mom says that's where we're having dinner tonight."

Something about his half-misery about his small hometown made me laugh. Mostly because it made me think about Dayton, Ohio, where I was from. It was a whole city trying to be upper-class and not quite making it there. Not even really getting close. His mock disdain for it was just one more thing we had in common, just one more thing that made me love him.

And there it was again, that word creeping into my thoughts, even though I'd tried to focus on things that would chase it away—the fact that we were in college, for one, and that I'd only known him for six weeks. The fact that when we were together we mostly ate and watched TV and had sex. We didn't have a history besides him being the fat kid at camp and me giving him a pity kiss, even though that was an eternity ago.

We pulled off the freeway about half an hour later, and the SUV handled the curving hill downward so beautifully that I could completely concentrate on watching the little town unfold before my eyes—a little network of white houses and golden-tipped churches huddled between the mountains and blanketed in mist.

"Oh, it's pretty!" I said, smiling and gripping his hand.

"You think so?" he asked, a bemused smile on his face.

"Yeah, I do. It's sweet. Kind of like a storybook. Why all the churches?"

"Super ethnic town.Lots of Polish and Italian Catholics. They love their churches more than their own houses."

My heart panged at that. "Everything in Ohio is flat, and kind of new. Not quite so many roots. More spread out. This is like a fairy tale."

"You really like it, huh?"

"I love it, actually," I said, looking up and meeting his eyes. His softened, and then he swallowed and cleared his throat.

"Good. Because no matter how different my mom is and how much I've grown up, this will always be home." He laughed a short laugh, and I squeezed his hand. "My house is...modest. You'll see. It's not that awesome, and I don't know what room Mom will have you in, and—"

I leaned in to kiss the underside of his jaw, which I knew drove him wild. "Will you be there?" I murmured.

A rough chuckle rolled up from his throat. "Of course, sweetheart. Anywhere you'll be."

"Then it's perfect."

We wound down through the streets of the small town, whose streets were crammed with tiny white houses, Masoniclodges, a few mom and pop diners, an elementary school and a high school, and churches. Churches everywhere. We pulled into the parking lot of the casino, which actually looked like a huge hotel, were it not for the signs telling us it was a casino. We walked inside, and the whole thing was filled with office-quality carpet and slot machines as far as the eye could see—none of the showgirls or flashing lights or lavish card dealer tables like you saw in the movies about Vegas. The lights weren't even dimmed. It was just a huge room filled with small-town people with nothing better to do. I couldn't help but smile.There was something really sweet about the whole thing.

A girl in a white shirt, tuxedo vest, and black bow tie carrying a tray with a half-empty drink walked up to us and asked, "Can I help you two?"

Nate's eyes darted around the room, suddenly wary. I squeezed his hand and smiled at the waitress. "Yes, thanks. We're looking for the restaurant?"

"Right this way," she said, sauntering off to the left. We crossed out of the huge room with the tacky patterned carpet and into a restaurant that looked like half the Italian chain restaurants I'd seen: side wall painted like a faux ancient brick you might see in Italy, if you squinted hard enough, bottles of cheap wine lining the walls, and Sinatra crooning over the speakers. I didn't know what about it made me grin, but it did.

Nate looked into my eyes, his expression bemused. "What?" he asked.

"I don't know. It reminds me of home, maybe. You have to admit, this is kind of cute. A good attempt, right?"

Now a grin broke out across his face. "We had like every special dinner growing up here. In the last ten years, this has been the nicest restaurant in town, and we weren't going to drive down to Philly, so..."

I stood up on tiptoes to kiss him. "It's perfect," I said, and I swear I felt his shoulders relax just standing next to me.

Just as I was pulling my lips from his, I heard the squeal.

"Natey!" A woman with huge blonde hair held up with what looked like half a can of hairspray, dramatic purple and blue eyeshadow framed with cat-eye eyeliner, and enough perfume to scent the whole restaurant scurried up to us on four-inch heels. Nate half rolled his eyes, smiled, and said under his breath, "I told you," before turning and wrapping his arms around his mom's shoulders and rocking back and forth as he hugged her tight.

Yeah, my heart swelled about twenty sizes when I saw that, and even a little more when he murmured, "Hey, Ma."

Okay, yeah. This was the guy for me. At that moment, I knew, hands down.

"And this must be Catherine?"

My stomach jumped. He'd used my full name when he talked to his mom about me? "Uh, yeah." I blushed. "Cat is fine."

"I'm Shelley," she said, smiling and stretching out her hand, which I shook. She leaned back to look at the two of us, and I stifled a grin when I realized she was wearing acid-washed jeans. Definitely a sweet lady, and definitely a blast from the past. And the bright red press-on nails were a nice touch.

"Well, he said you were beautiful, but I never would have thought…"

Just then, out of the corner of my eye, I swore I saw Nate give her a sharp look and a head shake, but she grabbed my shoulder before I could really look. "I never would have thought you were so stunning. You're a model in Philly, aren't you?"

"Well, I…" I stammered.

"Yes. She is. Actually, that's how we met."

My jaw dropped. I didn't plan on talking about nude me at this dinner, but I when I thought about it, it was okay.

"We're waiting for someone, right?" Nate asked.

"Yes, Rich is on his way. But he'sgonna be another fifteen minutes."

"Okay, so let's get a table, and I'll let Cat tell you all about it."

Ten minutes later, we'd gotten drinks and appetizers and I'd laid out the whole story about how Nate and I had met—first in camp, and then with me nude modeling. That felt like an eternity ago, now that I said it out loud. And I only left out one thing—the why. That is, until she asked.

"So how'd you end up in there, sweetheart?" My mouth dropped open, and I briefly considered telling her the whole sordid tale. She seemed like a lady who would understand, with her obvious attention to keeping up the way she looked. But just as I was about to say something, she waved down the waiter to ask for another glass of wine.

"Maybe wait until Rich gets here, Ma?" Nate said under his breath.

"Well maybe I did!" she smiled. "Look, here he comes!"

A guy in blue jeans, cowboy boots, and a striped button-down shirt came sauntering up to the table. Shelley stood and grinned, scooting out of the booth to wrap her arm around his waist. "Hey, baby."

Nate rolled his eyes, and I giggled and elbowed him. "Kids, this is Rich. Rich, baby, this is my handsome son Nate and his even more gorgeous girlfriend, Cat."

"Pleased to meet you." He said, scooting into the booth next to her and flashing a smile. He was handsome, with salt and pepper hair, and a chin dimple. But what really got me was the twang that ran through even the few short syllables he'd said. I could barely keep the amusement out of my voice when I asked, "So, you're not from here, huh?"

"No, hon, I'm not. Hard to hide, I guess." Rich spent the next half hour over appetizers, salads, and drinks for the two of them telling us how he'd come up to work on expanding the casino area, but how he usually worked as a real estate developer in Texas. "I'm trying to get this gorgeous girl to let me take her back there with me," he finished, leaning over to kiss her cheek.

Nate's eyes flared. "Are you serious?"

His mom gave a little nod and squirm in her seat, like she'd been sitting on the news and just waiting for the right time to pull it out. Nate shook his head, as if maybe he'd just heard wrong. "You guys have been together for…"

"A year now, Natey."

He gave a nervous laugh. "Yeah," he said. "I guess it has been."

"Oh, sweetie," Shelley reached across the table to place her hands on his, and Nate yanked back, sliding his arm around my back instead.

Her face fell, but didn't lose the relaxed, slightly happy expression. I counted mentally— how many glasses of wine had she had? Four? Yeah, and Rich had had as many glasses of beer to match.

"We'll talk about it later. Tomorrow."

Rich leaned over and whispered something in her ear. She nodded and giggled. "Speaking of tomorrow, is it okay if we see you two then? After dessert, of course. But Rich booked us a room here, and he's flying back down to Texas tomorrow, so we thought we'd stay here a little longer."

Nate just looked at her.

"I booked us a room. I hope y'all don't mind."

Then, Nate shook his head. "No, no, not at all." He cleared his throat, looked down, then flagged the waitress. "Could I just get a scotch? On the rocks? And maybe bring us some tiramisu, too."

My head darted to the side. Nate never drank. Wouldn't drink, or so he had told me.

"Nate, what…"

"Just one, sweetheart."

I didn't actually have a problem with it.It was just unlike him.

But when it came, Nate was as normal as ever, nudging the giant plate of tiramisu toward me more often than he attacked it with his own fork, and even offering me a drink of the scotch.

"Tastes incredible together," he said, but I wrinkled up my face.

"Remember the last time I drank?" I said it under my breath, since I didn't want to have that conversation with his mom and her boyfriend.But they were talking quietly between themselves anyway, lost in their own world. I grinned to myself, and nudged Nate. He hadn't finished his scotch yet, but I took the last bite of tiramisu, licking my lips and winking at him.

He definitely sat up at attention when I did that.

"We should get home, Mom. Cat's been up since this morning for an early class," Nate said to his mom, who nodded and smiled.

"Okay, babe. I'll be home bright and early so we can start on the pumpkin pie." She turned to me. "We bake from scratch every year. He's awesome at rolling the dough."

Well, if that wasn't the sweetest thing I'd ever heard. I might be falling even more in love with him.

We walked out to the car, and Nate opened my door, as always. There was a wet chill to the November air, but my body buzzed with knowing we were about to be all alone in the house, just the two of us. I was sure he would waste no time warming me up.

He started the car, then turned to me and took my face in both of his hands. He kissed me hungrily, and the sweet taste of the tiramisu mingled with the faint trace of alcohol left on his breath to something utterly delicious. My entire body was suddenly on edge. "You were incredible," he said, tucking an errant strand of hair back behind my ear.

I licked my lower lip, something I knew drove him absolutely wild. "What?" I asked innocently. "I liked her."

"Most girls... well, anyway. She loved you." He backed the car out of its spot, pulled out of the lot, and started down some winding back roads.

"You okay to drive?" I asked as he picked up speed.

"With all we had to eat? Totally."

He did seem to be in perfect control of the car, so I relaxed and enjoyed the feeling of his hand rubbing my knee, then slowly making its way up my thigh. His fingers were so long that they actually made my legs look shapely and cute instead of huge, and almost nothing could make me feel sexier.

We pulled up a hill and turned onto a little street full of little white houses with small yards. A narrow driveway separated two of them, and we pulled into it, next to a one-and-a-half-story with a flower box in the front and a bluebird painted on the mailbox.

"Oh my God." I said, grinning.

"It's not much…"

"It's absolutely adorable," I said.

"Home sweet home."

The back had a lattice-framed porch, and I watched his shoulders move even through his thick jacket as he climbed it, getting just high enough to reach over the top and undo a latch. Inside the porch, which looked like it served as a sort of a storage area and mudroom, he reached under an overturned flowerpot and pulled out a key. He propped open the screen door and unlocked the house, opening into a small kitchen housing an even smaller eating area.

"Well, it's not much, but I'll show you around..." He started flicking on lights.

But I couldn't stand it anymore. I grabbed the sleeve of his jacket, spun him around, and plunged my hands inside, gripping at his waist. "Only if we can start with the bedroom," I said, taking advantage of his surprise to crush my lips against his.

Half a minute later, our lips were still fused, but we'd both kicked our shoes off and he'd undone my bra and I'd unbuttoned his pants. Something about me was desperate to get my hands on him, and when I did, I was absolutely not sorry.

He was hard as a rock. And from the way his mouth was devouring my neck, then working its way along the edge of my bra after he hastily unbuttoned my blouse, he hadn't planned on starting anywhere else.

I pushed him away, laughing and gasping. "Seriously, though. Take me to bed, before we end up doing it on the table."

Mischief flickered in his eyes, and I'd almost never seen anything sexier, including him shirtless. There was something about a guy with that look in his eyes, combined with knowing what that guy could do to drive me absolutely wild, which turned me on like nothing else.

I hadn't meant it literally when I said "Take me to bed," but that's the way he took it. In an instant, he'd hitched my legs up around his waist, and started walking all one hundred and eighty pounds of me through the dark house with not a grimace or a grunt. We walked through what I thought was probably a living room, turned a tight corner, then he hoisted me up around his waist again. His lips never left mine as we climbed a flight of stairs, then went straight through a door and landed on a free-standing bed, on a plain metal frame in the middle of what was definitely his teenage bedroom.

It was so dark I could barely see the outline of a dresser holding a TV in one corner, some posters on the walls, and another small door that probably led to a bathroom. The house was warm, and not a single goosebump erupted on my skin as he tugged my shirt off my arms and laid me back on the soft sheets, his tongue already sliding under the edge of my bra, making me arch my back and whimper and squirm at the sheer pleasure of it.

I hooked my fingers into the waistband of my jeans, which he'd already somehow unbuttoned, and tugged them down, kicking them off so I could get my legs around his waist again. As soon as I did, I yanked his shirt up so that I could run my hands up over his shoulder muscles. Feeling them flex as his hands tugged my bra away from my breasts, then clutch at my waist as he licked and sucked every inch of them, drove me absolutely wild in a way nothing ever had before.

He was rock-solid against my leg, and when he finally kicked out of his own pants and he pressed up against me, the only thing I wanted, the only thing I could remember ever wanting, was him inside me, pumping into me, being completely and totally mine. I wanted all of him. Every bit of Nate, every discomfort and every fear I saw in his eyes.

I pulled his shirt over his head, and he pushed himself to sitting upright to tug in the rest of the way off. His hair stood up every which way, and between that, the hard lines of his torso in the dim light, and the wild flash of wanting in his eyes, I scrambled up to kneel, facing him.

He stroked the side of my face, kissing around my lips in four different places before diving in again. My fingers threaded back through his hair, clutching it, and he moaned. I almost didn't notice the sway of my breasts, so much bigger and less perky now than they had been before the accident, before they crushed up against his chest.

That seemed to set something off in him, because his hands dropped from my face to cup my breasts on either side, and he buried his face between them, kissing each one desperately before sucking one nipple into his mouth, drawing on it so hard that I cried out as the slightly painful pleasure shot through me.

He settled back on the bed so that his legs crossed Indian-style in front of him, and hitched my legs around his waist yet again. His hot length pressed into the sensitive space between my legs, which was now sopping wet. I didn't care. I needed all of him touching all of me, and I needed it now.

I captured his mouth with mine, raised up on both my knees, grabbed his steel shaft, and sank down on top of him.

"Oh, fuck," he moaned as his strong hands wrapped around my hips, guiding me up and down to take him in again and again. I was in heaven. He was so much deeper, more controlled, maybe, then when it was just him on top. His body touched more of mine than it ever had before, and it felt incredible. Like this was a secret no one else would ever have, something no one else could ever know.

He pumped into me, harder and more urgent each time. "Oh, sweetheart," he murmured as his mouth explored my neck, sucking at my skin and drinking it in like he'd never tasted anything so incredible. Then, even though I didn't think it was possible, he turned even harder inside me, and I cried out at the sheer sensation of it. "Holy shit," I managed between clenched teeth.

He grunted and, in one swift motion, had me on my back on top of the billowy comforters. His bicep flexed as he planted one hand on the side of my head and the other between my legs. "I was gonna go, sweetheart, and I want this to last just a little longer."

I nodded, biting my lip. His lips fluttered over my eyelids, down my neck, and licked all the way around my breast again. "These are the most gorgeous breasts I've ever seen," he growled, never letting his lips leave my skin, like it would kill him if he broke contact.

It might have killed me.

Then his tongue was tracing a hot trail down my stomach, swirling into my navel and making me writhe with anticipation. He had to stay on his path, I knew now, or I would die. Part of me wanted that tongue swirling around my clit, and the other part wanted him inside me, filling me, proving he was mine, again.

I cried out when his mouth moved between my legs, alternately sucking and tugging my soft wetness between his teeth. Just when I thought I couldn't stand not being filled by him one second longer, his fingers plunged into me, dipping in and out and stroking concentrated spots that had only gotten general attention from his thrusting.

All of a sudden, the orgasm hit me like a truck, flaring from a small point and brutally taking control of my whole body in a fraction of a second. I threw back my head and screamed, loving the knowledge that no upstairs or

downstairs neighbors would hear anything. This
night belonged to just me and Nate.

As I came down from my climax, a totally
new urge took over. Nate had made his way back
up to my mouth, but there was only one other
place I wanted mine to be now. "I want to suck
you," I growled against his lips, and it was my
turn to flip him on his back, straddle him, and
slowly lick my way across every inch of his
delicious pecs and abs. I wanted him in my
mouth. All of him.

The solid line separating his abs from his
hips was the tastiest, and I sucked every inch of
skin there, nipping it with my teeth on my slow
route down to where I knew he wanted me most.
When his silky soft hardness bumped my cheek, I
couldn't wait a second longer. I sucked him into
my mouth, swirling my tongue around the head
and thrilling at the tangy salt taste of him, ten
times hotter than my mouth. I grinned at the
groan that came from up above.

"Oh, sweetheart," he said as I took my turn
licking him up and down, chasing my lips with
my hand until he was harder to the touch than
even I could have ever imagined.

"Stop," he gasped, clutching my hair gently in his hand. "Stop it. You have to stop, or I'll…"

I lifted my head and smiled at him innocently.

"Oh, that's it, sweetheart. I need to be inside you. Now."

I squealed as he reached under my arms and clutched my shoulders, basically throwing me back on the bed and plunging into me without hesitation.

I let out a full-volume scream. God, it felt so good.

"I'm so sorry," he gasped.

"For what?" I half laughed, half moaned, as the incredible sensation of his hips grinding against mine washed over me.

"For going so fast. Just, after that, all I can think about is…." His voice trailed off, like he was ashamed of what he was about to say.

"Fucking me?" I finished, grinning and pausing to suck on his neck.

His forehead fell against my shoulder as he sighed. "Yeah."

"Well, stop thinking about it. Just do it."

He took one long hard, look at me, and then plunged into me harder than I ever thought possible. I cried out—couldn't help it. It was the strangest mix of pleasure and pain and pressure. I knew he was a big boy, but damn. It felt like he was touching, stretching, stroking every part of me, inside and out. The sheer sensation of it touched some place inside me that was wildly deeper and more sensitive than my clit ever could be, and another orgasm rocked through me, making every cell of my body tremble.

Just when I thought I couldn't keep going another second without flopping, exhausted, back onto the sheets, Nate slammed into me with one, two, three quick strokes. He let forth an earth-shattering cross between a groan and a growl, and then went still, his hot breath huffing against my neck.

"Jesus, Cat. Holy shit." He finally rolled off of me and we lay there for long minutes, kissing and grinning and laughing. Finally, he reached over me and grabbed a box of tissues from the nightstand. We cleaned up, rolled together under the sheets, and wove our bodies together. My hands couldn't stop roving over him, and the fact that he let me trail my fingertips over him, and returned the action, made drifting off to sleep in his arms almost as blissful as having him inside me.

Chapter 14

I woke with a start. There was no green-numbered glow of an alarm clock anywhere nearby, but the lightening indigo of the sky I spied out of the one crack between the curtain and the window told me that sunrise would be soon, and I had no idea how long it would be before Nate's mom got back. I fumbled through the dresser drawers in his room, finally pulling out a t-shirt that looked like it would be a tent on me. *Wilkes-Barre lacrosse*, it said, and I grinned at this relic from Nate's childhood. Somehow, the more time I spent in this house, the more love I felt for him, and the more I wanted my story to be completely a part of his.

I felt a pang of sadness that I hadn't told him last night how I felt, but when I remembered the amazing sex we'd had, I realized I didn't really regret it. There would be more time.

As I pulled the shirt down over my head, and found some boxers in another drawer—a size large, I realized, even though he wore a medium now—I found my way to the bathroom. Thank God for his mom—she had a normal selection of face and body washes to allow me to clean up. I even found a spare toothbrush, still in its package, and I promised to replace it the next day when I could get away to a drugstore.

Twenty minutes later, I'd made a pot of coffee, rushed out to the car to grab my suitcase, and gotten into some stretchy jeans and a sweater that actually made me feel cute. I sat there on the couch in his mom's small living room, browsing through the newspaper that had magically landed on their front step that morning, wondering what Nate was going to tell his mom about where I'd slept, and grinning at the thought of him stammering his way through an excuse.

I leaned back on the couch and soaked up the feeling of being in his childhood home. My eye caught on a small bookshelf in the corner, and what looked like a row of yearbooks and photo albums on one of the shelves.

Oh my God. I had to see this. A huge part of me actually really wanted to see fat-kid Nathaniel West. I didn't know whether it was to relive that time at camp, to gloat to myself over how gorgeous and buff he was now, or to feel a little better about myself being less than thin. Which, I now realized, I hadn't thought of for a single second last night. I grinned at the realization. My hands brushed over the fake leather spines with gold embossed lettering. I grinned as I did the calculations. This was one was from ten years ago. The year I would have met him at camp.

I flipped through the glossy pages, chuckling at the ridiculous gelled hairstyles and graphic tees the boys wore. Buck teeth, ridiculous amounts of freckles, and bodies too scrawny for their shirts lined page after page. I got through most of them before I arrived at the "W"s. There he was. I gasped, and my hand flew up to cover my mouth, hoping to stifle the giggle that bubbled up there.

I wasn't laughing because I was making fun of him—no, it was mostly because the craziest thing was that I could see Nate—the one I knew now. I could see the sparkle in his eyes and the way his mouth quirked into a half-smile when he was trying to look cute. He was adorable. And I could totally see what it was about him that made me do more than laugh at him when I pulled his name for Seven Minutes in Heaven, ten years ago at summer camp. I flipped it closed, then before putting it away, flipped to the inside back cover. A bunch of signatures scrawled in bubblykid-handwriting scattered across the blue-paper covered hardcover.

I shelved the yearbook and picked up the next one on the shelf, from two years later. It was obvious that Nate had gotten a little taller, and had some clue of what to do with his hair, but he was still ridiculously pudgy. A swoop of fat circled his jaw, and I brushed my fingers against the picture, trying to see how this little boy would turn into the man I knew so intimately. The one I wanted to be around all the time. I flipped to the back page of this yearbook too, and there were far fewer signatures for this year. I frowned.

I turned back to the page with his picture, and examined it again. He was pretty geeky, but not so very different-looking from any of the other guys. There was something different about this year's picture, though. The sparkle was gone from his eyes, replaced by something harder, more distant.

I pushed the book back into place and pulled out the next one. This time, I flipped to the back cover first. Almost no signatures, except for a couple scrawled *Stay Cools* and *See you next years*.

The picture of Nate—whose name actually said "Nate" now, not "Nathaniel" made me gasp. In the two years since the last photo, he'd grown eight inches, maybe ten. And, by the looks of it, hadn't gained a pound. Same eyes, same cheekbones, now visible without the fat hanging off of them. A hint of the jawline he'd have four years from then, just rounder with youth. And, I noticed as I cocked my head to the side, he was trying to clench it, make it look harder. Stronger.

Something had made him really, really angry in the two years before this picture was taken, and I was willing to bet it had something to do with the lack of signatures in the back cover.

That was the last yearbook on the shelf, which made sense. None for his senior year, but I wouldn't have gotten one either if basically no one had signed the inside of last year's.

Getting people to sign a yearbook was basically the entire reason for buying one in the first place. I knew that well enough, since mine had been filled every year. Part and parcel of transforming from the skinny stick bug in ninth grade to the only girl at school who was a model.

Seemed that Nate and I had both had a weird time of transformation in high school. The only difference was that mine had become more bearable while his seemed to have been much, much less.

I ran my hands over the rest of the books on the shelf. Photo albums, it looked like. I pulled one out and flipped through pictures of Nate as a baby—taking baths in the sink, learning how to hold a baseball bat when he was so tiny the bat itself was bigger than he was. A tall man, rippling with muscles, held the bat while Nate rested his hands over the man's. Must have been his dad.

On the next page, there was a much larger picture, and this time Nate must have been four or five, He was sitting on the man's lap, cradled in his arms, with solid, round arm muscles. The next thing I noticed after Nate himself was his dad's face—and how much he looked exactly like his father.

I flipped the page again. More photos of Nate and his dad, at an arcade, hiking, in the kitchen. The resemblance between Nate and his dad was so striking, it was almost as though I was looking at photos of Nate with a child.

And then, two pages later, Nate looked suddenly older, and had started to round out into the fat kid Nate I knew. There were pictures of him playing with Legos, reading a book, posing with a dog. But the absence of photos with his father was too conspicuous. I knew what I would find when I turned the page.

A photo of Nate and his dad on a California beach. It looked like summer, the way everyone around them was wearing a swimsuit and the sun glinted off the water in blinding, diamond sparks. But the most obvious difference between this photo and the others was the way Nate and his dad stood—about six inches apart, arms crossed over chests. Nate smiled, but it wasn't the same sweet-little-boy smile in all the pictures before. And not the same smile I saw when Nate and I spent hours under the covers, talking and kissing and grinning at each other.

The last photo album I pulled wasn't nearly as organized. There were a few pictures of pudgy Nate, then fat Nate. A bunch of them had his hand in front of the camera, and it looked like somewhere around age fourteen, Shelley had just given up on taking photos of him. I didn't blame her.

Stuffed in the pages, too, were a few random things—birthday cards from grandparents, ticket stubs from baseball games. Newspaper clippings, where Nate's name was listed at the bottom of an article about the junior high lacrosse team, at the bottom under *Members not mentioned*. No plane ticket stubs, no more pictures with Dad.

Then, a picture with Nate's dad sitting next to a hospital bed, his arm around a beautiful blonde woman who couldn't have been more than a few years older than me.And holding a newborn baby.

I'd bet a thousand bucks Nate had a baby half brother or sister out in California that he wasn't telling me about, and that his dad having a brand new family so far away was a big part of what had been pissing him off in that yearbook photo.

I flipped the page, and saw a picture of tall, but thin, Nate, in a graduation gown, in front of his high school. His mom had the big hair and press-on nails and a dress that was maybe a bit too short. She looked ecstatic, and Nate looked annoyed. A hint of a smile was there, though, and I saw that same expression he'd had last night—he loved his mom, and he was tolerating what he saw as her antics. It was actually pretty sweet.

I flipped the page, and there was a stack of white papers folded in half and stuck inside. I was just about to unfold them, when another stack of pictures fell out. They were all of Nate shirtless. This must have been the bodybuilding thing he was telling me about.

Sure enough, each photo had a black background from what looked like it must have been a competition. In the first one in the stack, he looked like a slightly buffed-up version of thin high-school Nate. I could see the shadow of the sides of his abs, and his shoulders starting to round out. I flipped the photo. His mom had dated it October of three years ago—our freshman year. I grinned, eagerly flipping through even more.

Four photos in, I'd seen the incredible transformation from skinny Nate to buff Nate— the Nate I knew, and couldn't keep my hands off of every time he pulled his shirt off. Or I saw his muscles under his shirt at all. It was those delicious cut abs, traveling down over his hips and pointing straight to my latest favorite part of him. It was a little weird to see his skin get darker, and progressively shinier in the pictures, but I figured that was normal for a bodybuilder.

No big deal. That one was dated June at the end of our freshman year.

The next picture, though, wasn't just a little weird. It was really weird.

It featured Nate standing against one of those backdrops, but this time he was in a really serious bodybuilding pose. His skin was even darker and more oiled up than it had been in the other pictures, and his expression just looked….distant. Solid, and angry. No hint of a smile, no spark to the eyes. Nothing.

But the freakiest thing was the veins. Veins everywhere. They popped out of his biceps, shoulders, and neck, and they made my gorgeous Nate look gross.

That was the last picture in the stack, dated October of our sophomore year. The transformation in just a year was completely insane.

A thought flitted through my head. No way anyone was building that much muscle that fast unless—

I shook my head, trying to clear it of the thought. Nate would never have done steroids. Besides, even if he had, he didn't look anything like that now. Sure, he was built, and hard-cut, and he worked out, but no more than an hour or so a day. And he ate normally, too. He was normal.

Now I was really curious about what was on those papers, though. I unfolded the stack of about twenty pages, all of them printouts from the same website—collegebodybuilder.com. The first article was called *College Bodybuilding – First Steps*, and sure enough, *by Nate West, USC*.

A smile flitted across my face as I read his somewhat clumsy writing outlining the differences between being in college and high school, and how bodybuilding could add some discipline to your routine. The thing that really got me was the last paragraph:

College is your chance to become someone different from who you always were. My whole life, I was the fat, dorky kid who no one ever wanted to talk to. College is my chance to form my body into something different, in a place where no one knows who I used to be. There's no such thing as the old Nate.

I frowned a little bit and flipped to the next one. This one was called: *The College Bodybuilding Life – All One Discipline*. This one talked about how showing up to the gym every day and working on reaching your bodybuilding goals wasn't so different from reaching your academic goals. One line said: Some people think I'm crazy for spending three hours every day in the gym. But they'd never call me nuts for spending twice that much time studying – which I do. As an architecture major, I'm just as dedicated to learning about the structure of buildings as I am to maintaining and building a sound structure for my body.

Three hours? Every day? No way, that wasn't my Nate. He must have had, like, no life. I checked the comments at the bottom. Whereas there had been six on his first article, this one had exploded to fifty-seven—and from the first few that showed up on the bottom of the final page of the article, they were people who knew him. Friends. Names I'd never heard about.

Now that I thought of it, Nate never talked about his friends back home. Never texted, never e-mailed or Skyped with them.

If I had any doubt as to whether they existed, though, back at USC, the next article would prove me wrong. The title of this one was *Balancing Your Gym Life and Your Social Life*.

Most body builders stay away from partying, but this college boy loves to spend a night out. And even though I'm too young to drink (and the commenters can keep their naysaying to themselves, I know where you live, little bitches) I know that some well respected body builders will enjoy a night out on the town every now and then. Four, six, eight beers – as long as you can get yourself home and you know you'll be safe (wink wink nudge nudge) then it's no problem.

Underneath this article by Nate, who was apparently a total asshole the day he wrote it, was a picture of him standing in a bar. He was wearing a tight gray t-shirt with muscles even bigger than the ones he had now, straining underneath. He held a beer in each hand, and each arm was wrapped around a girl. One was taller than he was, and one was just an inch or so shorter.

And they were both thin as freaking rails. The tall one had her midriff bare, and even in the grainy printed picture, I could see her hipbone jutting out.

My stomach twisted. Nate had never said he liked bigger girls, but I guessed after all our time together, I'd just assumed…

And then my eyes landed on the photo caption:

Writer Nate West enjoys a night on the town with his girlfriend and her friends. "My girl is the hottest on campus," West said. "I like a girl I can get my hands around."

My world spun around me, and I thought I would be sick. But there was one more article left. My hands trembled as I flipped to it, because somehow, I knew what would be there. It was titled: *Fat is not Fit, and Overweight is Not Fabulous – a response to the USC Observer's Plus Size Model Spread*. My head spun, but I kept reading.

Of course POSE magazine, USC's publication by fashion students, can be easily found lying around campus, and this was the first one I'd bothered picking up to read. If it was possible, I was both horrified and glad I had.

On the cover was an intriguing descriptor – "The Real Woman Issue." Being into fitness, I thought I might flip the page to see some practical gym outfits for girls or something – maybe I'd buy one for my girlfriend. Inside, I was appalled by what I saw.

The entire centerfold was comprised of poses by nude, plus sized models. The fact that they were nude wasn't what bothered me, though – it was the fact that this was what we were defining, on USC's campus, as the quintessential 'real woman.'

These girls have rolls on their stomachs and sagging under their arms – they're not real women, they're unhealthy women. I understand that some people are plus-sized, and that's normal for them, but I don't think a publication for college students should be glorifying this body type. Big bones don't make these girls that way – big meals do. It's a bad example for our student population, and if flies in the face of all the hard work fitness organizations are doing to ensure a healthy student body. What kind of role models are we showing the USC population? Or high school girls, who are thinking about maybe attending USC? What message does it send?

I know that most people won't read this article, but I just wanted to say – I'm not discriminating against people who have some weight to lose, and I encourage them to work hard to do so. That's one of my missions on this campus. And as such, I don't think they have any business being naked in a magazine.

Studies show that calling overweight people out for being unhealthy can spur them to change their lives. And to whatever extent this little piece does that, I hope it makes these girls and anyone admire their unhealthy bodies realize - It's not art, it's a display of what happens when you don't take care of yourself. And until these girls can do so, they should get in the gym and off the pages of a magazine that represents our entire school.

Sincerely, a concerned Trojan.

The article ran only left a little bit of room at the bottom of the page for comments, but through my welling tears I read the two that were there. One said, *Preach on, brother*, and the other said, *You are an ignorant asshole*.

Yep. I totally agreed with that last one. Nate was an ignorant asshole. An ignorant asshole I'd been sleeping with, been falling in love with, for the last three months.

Absolutely nothing felt like it made sense. My stomach churned and the room spun around me. If I thought I could have made it to the bathroom to throw up, I would have. Instead, I found my phone on the couch beside me and, with shaking fingers, texted Joey.

- **Need to get out of here. Now.**
- *LolWhat happened?*
- **I'll fill you in. But I'm up here in Wilkes Barre, no car. What do I do?**
- *Holy shit. You're not joking. Hold on.*

Fifteen seconds later, another text popped up with a phone number.

- *Call these guys. They'll come get you. I'll book you a car from here.*

My eyes filled with tears. I held down the number, clicked "call," and breathed out a sigh of relief when the recorded greeting for a rental car place came over the phone. I stepped outside, phone pressed to my ear, and thanked God I could see both a street sign and the house number without leaving the front porch. With a shaky voice, I gave the tired-sounded guy on the other end the address.

"We'll be there in five minutes. You're just around the corner."

It took me less than thirty seconds to find my jacket and stuff everything I'd brought back in my suitcase. I was so grateful I'd packed light at that moment, because I didn't want to leave anything in Nate's car.

In the last few minutes before the rental car guy got there, I debated going back upstairs to look at Nate sleeping. But when my eyes flicked outside and saw the sun coming up, I knew with absolute certainty that I never wanted to see that ignorant asshole again.

The rental car guy tried to chat, as I signed the papers, but I just wasn't in the mood to talk with him about why I was leaving this house— which he assumed was my parents'—at seven-thirty on Thanksgiving morning. Everything was still spinning around me, and tears still filled my eyes every few seconds, but I swiped them angrily away. As soon as I felt that burn of anger start to edge out the twisting in my stomach, I felt a little better, and I spent the entire drive back to the turnpike, pressing my foot all the way to the floor to make it up the steep, windy mountain in the little hatchback, concentrating on that anger, letting it consume me.

Nate's article from less than a year ago at USC not only said everything I'd been freaking out about since my accident. That much, I'd seen. That much, I could handle.

But there was no fucking way I believed a guy could change from this jerkwad on the page to a guy who really truly thought I was beautiful and gorgeous, inside and out. All the things he had said when we were together, about how real women looked this way, about how beautiful I was…they were all lies.

It really didn't make sense. Why he would have kissed me like he did that first time, or tried so hard to get my number, or taken me rock climbing?Why couldn't he keep his hands off me on that first official date? None of it made sense—not the way he looked at my body in awe, or encouraged me to eat dessert when we both knew I shouldn't.

The guy who wrote that article could not possibly be the same guy who made me feel so beautiful and loved.

And yet he was. And I had slept with him. A lot. And almost told him I loved him.

I did love him, in the world that was this morning, I told myself. But who did he think he was, fucking with my head so thoroughly? My thoughts swirled and my heart raced as I barreled down the turnpike in the little car, staring at each mile marker and willing the numbers to go down faster.

Nothing in this entire world made sense. I didn't know whether I was ugly or gorgeous, couldn't make sense of every single moment I'd spent with Nate. Didn't know if he was wonderful and this was all a dream, or if he was really an asshole that I'd somehow been lucky enough to figure out before I fell for his shit.

My phone buzzed about every ten minutes, and I knew it was Joey, but I also knew that there was no way I should be holding a phone to my ear driving at this speed in this mood. I picked up my phone and quickly texted her:

- **On my way back. ETA 10:00.**
- *Great. Dinner in Marion at 2:00. You're telling me what happened, cleaning up, and coming with.*

A huge lump rose in my throat. Things were finally feeling real. Probably because texting with Joey told me, for certain, that this was not a dream. I was going to have to go talk to my best friend, the one I'd basically ditched for the past two months, and tell her all about how I'd finally got back to feeling good about myself, only to find out that my boyfriend hated fat girls. Girls like me.

Chapter 15

I pulled off the turnpike onto the Schuylkill Expressway, winding around the first treacherous turn so slowly that the car behind me honked. "Shut up, asshole," I murmured under my breath. I wanted to purposely go even slower when we hit the main road, but Philadelphians and their road rage were nothing to fool around with.

In less than twenty minutes, I was pulling off onto 30th Street, and marveling at how different the University streets were without traffic. It really was like a different world, an alternate universe. So different-looking, I could almost believe the last twenty-four hours hadn't happened.

The last two months were a little harder to explain away.

I wound down the University streets, past Penn and Drexel, trying my hardest not to glance at the building that held Nate's apartment on my way to ours.

When I pulled up to my building, I was relieved to see Joey's face in the window, watching for me, and that just brought a whole fresh crop of tears. I saw her lift her phone to her ear, and then I stepped out of the car, feeling the air whipping against my face and freezing the tears into half-solid tracks on my cheeks. I wrenched my suitcase out of the car, grateful for half a second for all the rock climbing and weight training Nate had convinced me to do. It was light as a feather.

I trudged up to the front step, and Joey was waiting with the front door open. I heard her say, "Yes, pickup any time between now and one-thirty is fine. Thanks."

"Joey," I half-whined, half moaned. "You didn't have to do that."

"Yes, I did. I know you're broke as a joke, and leaving Nate at seven-thirty in the morning on Thanksgiving means you're not fucking around. And really, it's no big deal. It's probably better spent on you instead of having that huge post-finals party here like we were going to, anyway."

I stared around the apartment. We had a cleaning schedule, and it looked like the other three girls had actually stuck to it while I had been mostly absent since we moved in. It probably was better, but that didn't stop me feeling like shit for ruining plans for the girls that, by all accounts, were my best friends on campus. Shit.

I left my suitcase at the door and trudged over to the couch, just like I'd done that first day back when none of my clothes fit. Ridiculous how, back then, I thought that was the worst problem possible.

"Spill." Joey plopped down next to me. For the first time, I noticed how even her tiny body made the couch shake too.

"So. Nate."

"Yeah. What did he do? He was SO into you. It was obvious."

"Well, I found some old stuff of his." I explained the whole thing to her, detailing the articles and photos, the tears really streaming down my cheeks until by the end I was sobbing, snotting, and gulping for breath.

Joey punctuated my retelling with the appropriate "Holy shit," or shocked or sad face, and when I'd finally finished my story, launched herself off the couch and came back with a roll of toilet paper. "Sorry," she said sheepishly. "We're out of tissues."

I laughed, for the first time in hours.

"No, it's fine. I mean, it's basically the same thing."

"Yeah, and cheaper. Leaves more in the party fund, which you are going to desperately need."

I shook my head. "Nuh-uh. Not after the last time. Do you remember how trashed I got?"

"Yeah, but Nate didn't seem to care—"

My face fell.

Joey reached over to me as I started sobbing all over again. "Oh, I'm so sorry, honey," she said into my hair. "I'm so sorry. I didn't mean to—"

"No, that's the thing!" I wailed. "He didn't care. I mean, he told me I was gorgeous. He fucked me like I was gorgeous."

"Really? I mean, we haven't talked that much, but the sex, it was that good?"

I memory shot through me. Had it only been twelve hours ago that he'd been inside me and I'd sworn I'd never felt anything so incredible? Never would feel anything so incredible ever again?

The thought just made me wail even harder. "I wish I'd never gone snooping around his stupid house. Then I never would have seen that stupid article, and I never would know, and he'd keep being perfect forever and ever."

"Oh, honey. But you would have found out. You would have found out sometime, you know? And it could have been worse. It could have been in front of his whole family, or you could have met some of his friends from back home, or…."

I nodded numbly, staring off into the distance. "Just…I can't believe I was so fooled, you know? And why the hell would he have been so awesome if that's really how he feels?"

"Is it possible that he changed?"

"Since a year ago?From that colossal of an asshole?"

"I mean, he was in that nude-models class. And he did transfer."

Just then, my phone trilled Nate's ringtone. "Motherfucker," I muttered, willing the tears not to start up again as I hoisted myself up off the couch to get the phone. But Joey was hot on my heels.

"No. Let me handle that."

I opened my mouth to speak, but it was too late. Joey had snatched the phone from my hand. She stood there with her hand on a popped-out hip, the embodiment of attitude, as she pressed it to her ear. "Nate," she said in a sickly sweet voice. "Uh-huh. This is Joey." A pause. "No, Cat left as soon as she found evidence of what a dickwad you are." She grinned and stifled a laugh. "Okay. Happy fucking Thanksgiving, asshole."

"What did he say?" I asked. My heart pounded in my chest.

Joey looked at me with shifty eyes. "He was clueless. Do you mean to tell me you didn't even talk to him before you left?"

"Yeah, I mean he was still sleeping, so…"

"Well, I guess he'll probably call back once he figures out what you saw, huh?"

"I guess so." It wouldn't be too hard. I had left that last photo album's contents strewn across the coffee table, with the last article on top.

"He talked about my body so much, I should have known something was up. I just…I don't know. I felt like such shit about myself that I ate it up, you know?"

"Okay, but that just makes sense. Of course you wanted to hear you were gorgeous."

"And of course you guys telling me wasn't enough. Shit, Joey. I'm so sorry."

"Will you stop being stupid? You're going through an epic breakup, and I am your friend no matter what."

The words "epic breakup" hit me like a Mack truck. Somehow, in the last few hours, I hadn't thought of this as exactly what it was—my boyfriend was a douche, and I was breaking up with him.

The phone rang again, Nate's ringtone. God, I would hate that little tune forever.

Joey answered it again, and I heard Nate's voice on the other end, frantic. God, if I could hear it, he must be really upset. No. No. He's just embarrassed, and he didn't want to lose the easy fuck buddy he had in you. Pull yourself together.

Every part of me screamed that we weren't just fuck buddies. There was something different about us, something more.

Something that could never be the same again.

Joey's shrill laugh rang through the air, interrupting my thoughts. "You think I'm going to let you talk to her? Oh, that's hilarious."

I lunged for the phone. All thought was lost, and my body took over. My fat, unhealthy body, according to asshole-USC-Nate from another world.

"What?" I spat when I got the phone out of Joey's hand and against my ear.

"Cat. Cat, sweetheart, I don't…holy shit, you have to let me explain."

"I don't have to let you do anything."

But he kept talking anyway. "That was from a long time ago, I…"

"Nate, that was from one year ago. One year is not a long time. In any universe."

"Yeah, but Cat, things are different."

"By 'things,' you mean you fucked an ugly fat girl and now you'd like to be a little nicer?"

"If you'd just…can I see you, at least?" His voice broke.

"I really don't think so, Nate. I have to get well again. I'm sick of feeling like shit about myself. And every time I see you I'm just going to think about what you wrote in that article, and especially the way you told me not to do that Real Women Project thing here…I really don't think you're good for me at all." My voice was barely above a whisper as I spoke the last sentence.

The thing was, my body thought differently. My chest twisted and I felt sick. That didn't make a damn bit of difference to my destroyed feelings and Joey standing there supporting me and me no longer being in the same house with him, let alone in bed with that gorgeous naked body.

I took a deep breath. Yeah. I definitely needed some distance.

"Please, sweetheart, I don't even…" Nate blew out a long breath. "I want to explain."

"I don't think so. Don't call this number again." I hung up, trembling so hard I had to sit down again. I rested my elbows on my legs and put my head between my knees, breathing deeply. I vaguely noticed a knock on the door and sort of remembered pointing to my purse when Joey asked for the keys to the rental to give the guys, who had come to pick it up. Then the door closed and she was there again, rubbing my back and stroking my hair.

"You need to cry anymore?" she asked after a few long moments.

I blew out a shuddering breath. "No, I actually think I'm good."

"Good. Because we are going to clean you up, get you ready, and transfer you," she said, hopping up on and reaching both hands down to help me up, "to the couch at my parents' house, where Mom will make you coffee and you can eat as little or as much as you want, and we will all watch stupid Christmas movies and play pointless board games and everything will be perfectly wonderful. Okay?"

I cracked a smile. "Okay."

The awful thing about Thanksgiving at Joey's was that her mom dried out the turkey beyond recognition. The wonderful thing was that the mashed potatoes and pie were to die for. Later that night, we'd finally made it back to the sorority house,and were celebrating the end of the insane day with a bottle of wine. The crying had completely exhausted me, but while Joey and her little brothers had to set the table and help their mom clean up the kitchen, she let me lay down in the guest room and I had a three-hour nap.

Nate was on my mind constantly, of course. It only made sense. Mostly because, while he'd respected my request not to call my number again, he'd been texting me all damn day.

I know you're upset, but I just need to talk to you.

You have to believe me, sweetheart, that wasn't me. Not really.

Please just…call me.

There were about twenty like that. But every time I imagined calling him, talking to him, figuring out where he was and rushing to be near him, I couldn't figure out what I would say. I couldn't even figure out what my feelings were. I loved him, but every time I thought about those toxic, stupid sentences I'd read, and that dick look on his face in that last bodybuilding picture, I convinced myself that my loving him had to stop. No question.

Even though I had no idea how to make that happen.

Chapter 16

I continued ignoring texts from Nate all weekend, and I hovered around Joey to keep myself from breaking. She teased me about it, all the while coming up with stuff for us to do to fill the meager amount of time left until finals.

I was just fine with my Math and English finals, but it was my fashion design final that was absolutely killing me. It probably had to do with the fact that I was completely avoiding finding any models, and all my friends were too short or too curvy or both to fit the bill. As a result, I'd designed every outfit on a freaking mannequin, totally defeating the purpose of the project— design clothing that was shocking and could actually be worn. As many points for creativity as for wearability.

I was screwed.

I was shuffling through my portfolio on Sunday night, hoping to dig up some sketches I'd done when my head was clearer. Before I'd done the stupid nude modeling and had the gall to think that any guy on this stupid college campus would genuinely want to have a relationship with me, let alone fall in love with me. Before my head had been filled with working out and learning to enjoy life after my accident.

As I dug some stray scraps of paper out of the bottom of my huge portfolio, a thick, glossy tri-fold thunked to the floor. When I read the wording on it, the tears flooded my eyes again— they hadn't for days. Dammit.

REAL WORLD.REAL WOMEN. Design competition for clothing sized 12-18.

I blinked back the tears. This is the thing that had sparked my interest all the way back in the first week since I'd met Nate. But I couldn't have done it then, not really. Then, I didn't see my body as a canvas, as a gorgeous work of art, except for when Nate was telling me in real time.

But all those weeks with Nate, however fake they might have been, did do one thing for me. Whether the rest of the world saw me that way, I knew now that I was strong, and I was beautiful, just the way I was.

And girls like me needed gorgeous clothes too.

I stuffed everything I'd done all semester back in my portfolio.

As I frantically sketched, I realized that what Nate had told me the very first time we were together was absolutely true, and I could only see it now that it was laid out in front of me in a form grid, in black and white. I was not only beautiful—I was as close to mathematically, architecturally perfect as you could get.

I double- and triple-checked my measurements, and then, for the next week, I basically moved into the studio.

A week later, I'd scoured every nook and cranny of the design studio, as well as spent hours with the scissors, tissue-paper patterns, and sewing machines. The students who signed people in and out of the studio started bringing me coffee.

That Friday, I squeezed in an appointment with Doctor Albright. She was the only one who I wanted to share this project with before I shared it with everyone, for two reasons. First, she'd been right about Nate not being a guaranteed presence in my life, about not needing him to give me my self-worth, and I didn't want her to think that was lost on me. But second, and most importantly, I wanted her to see how far I'd come—from hating myself and feeling trapped in my own skin to accepting that I was beautiful like this too, and using my design talents to make myself look gorgeous in a way only I could.

I moved the box of tissues and knickknacks from her coffee table and spread out my design sketches. She looked at them and beamed at me. "You decided to do it. What made you decide?"

"I realized that I don't want to have to count on anyone to take care of me except me, including my body image. And if being taken care of doesn't mean having a fabulous wardrobe, then..."

"What's the point?" She laughed. "I couldn't agree more. I'm so proud of you, Cat."

The truth was, I was probably more proud of myself than anyone. And in that moment, I realized that I had needed that more than anything.

By Sunday, I'd turned the sound off on my phone, and Nate's texts got less and less frequent. His last one said simply, I don't want to give up. But I don't want to be a creep. I'm still coming to the show, but only because I want you to know how much I support you. Always have.

It was the only one I replied to. I couldn't help myself as my fingers flew over the touch screen. No you don't. Trust me.

I do. If I come, will you freak out?

Do what you want. It's a free country. Then, as soon as I'd hit send,

We're not hanging out.

No hanging out. Got it.

I stared at my studio table, strewn with fabric scraps and coffee cups, and then looked over at the mannequin I'd hacked to reflect my measurements.

I'd turned this studio upside down. And I'd turned myself around in the process.

The same suitcase that I'd brought to Nate's mom's house for Thanksgiving sat in the corner. I set to work carefully folding and tucking the outfits into the suitcase, taking care to keep all the pieces together.

Like I'd finally stitched the pieces of my life back together. Despite my accident.Despite Nate's lies. I was finally happy in this skin. Strong enough to finally love myself, no matter what size I wore.And even better? Proud of what I'd accomplished.Tomorrow was going to be awesome. I hoped.

The next morning, I wheeled the suitcase behind me with one hand and holding a duffle bag full of curling irons, steamers, and seven different pairs of shoes, among other things. Joey scurried to keep up with me while holding two steaming cups of coffee.

"Oh my God, Cat, this is so freaking exciting. I can't believe you never took me to one of your modeling things! I mean seriously, this is too much fun!"

I looked over at her, rolled my eyes, but then smiled wide. "Thanks for coming with me. Seriously. I never thought I'd be doing this again."

It still wasn't modeling like I used to do—Piper was one of our sorority sisters, who also happened to be a photography major and amazing at studio work. When I found out she'd be able to use photographing parts of my final application for credit in one of her classes, it pretty much sealed the deal.

I was going to design outfits for the Real Woman Challenge, and I was going to be my own model.

The only thing I had never anticipated was that I would be, in every way, the absolutely perfect person for the job.

Piper smiled wide when I arrived in the studio, showing me the curtained changing area and helping me hang up my outfits. She oohed and ahhed over each one, and helped me separate denim from silk from wool, deciding on the perfect plain-colored background for each.

I stepped into my first outfit, dark skinny jeans, red patent leather stilettos to die for—which I could never actually walk in, but were perfect for a photo shoot where I didn't actually walk anywhere, and a white silk top that dipped and draped in swoops that accented my breasts, showed off my toned shoulder muscles, and nipped in at my upper waist. I looked like a goddess, and I knew it.

"Shit," breathed Piper and Joey at the same time. "You're stunning."

Piper held her fancy camera so casually it might as well have been a hairbrush. "Okay. Just stand on the mat. You know the drill, right?"

"I do," I smiled. I'd done my hair in large, soft waves, and I loved the way they felt brushing across my cheekbones and teasing at my neck. I looked hot, size fourteen body and all.

Piper smashed her eye up to the camera and peered inside. "Just gonna run some test shots, okay? Give me some poses."

And so I did. I leaned over ever so slightly, made my lips pouty. I pushed my hands back through my hair and twisted at my waist.

"Yes, yes, Cat. Gorgeous. Give me more of that." The camera was snapping away and I hadn't really realized how much I had missed it. But I had. A lot.

Suddenly, that feeling surged through me again, for the first time in a year. The power of being absolutely beautiful, of being capable of being admired, and of being wanted, was so strong that I could barely stand it. And it had nothing to do with my weight and everything to do with my attitude. A grin stretched across my face.

"Incredible, Cat!" Piper seemed to love that, the show of genuine emotion. "Jesus, you are stunning."

I tried to remember if I'd ever used that true smile anywhere since the accident, except under the covers with Nate.

Nate. Shit.

Knowing he was bad for me was very different than the memories and emotions that told me just how badly I missed him every single minute. The tears welled in my eyes again, but I willed them to go back. Nothing was going to ruin this shoot. Nothing.

But it did remind me of the most important thing of this whole project, which was not me looking hot in stilettos.

"Hey, Joey. Would you grab those big white cards from my suitcase?"

This was the project—Project Real Woman. I was at the center of it, and I was going to make it the best damn thing these judges had ever seen.

Chapter 17

The huge auditorium at the center of Temple's campus had been completely transformed into a Paris runway. Hundreds of chairs lined a long, sleek platform that ended in a black curtain. Lights were rigged to showcase the incredible creations of the student designers.

I'd waited two years to finally have the privilege of helping construct some of the fashions that would go on the models that Temple brought in from as far away as Manhattan. And now I had chosen not to. I had to admit I felt a pang in my heart when I saw some of the truly gorgeous designs of my classmates coming down the runway—wild creations made entirely out of red feathers, or understated but structurally astounding outfits made out of strange combinations like black gauze and tweed.

As beautiful as the clothes were, it was strange to watch the girls wearing them. I'd spent so much time being told that I was beautiful when I looked like they did, feeling comfortable in a stick-thin body that, as it turned out, wasn't actually the body that looked best on me.

I'd done a pretty good job, between physical therapy and climbing and walking with Nate, at getting my leg back into shape. If I wore the right shoes, it hardly even hurt anymore.

I could have gone back to the hardcore workouts and the barely-eating that had kept me in top shape for the teen model competitions in high school and the runway jobs in college, the kind of calorie counting that had kept my Philadelphia agent happy. But the satisfaction of being stick-thin and only focused on how I looked had lost its appeal when I was with Nate.

Nate had helped me realize that I wasn't most attractive when I looked like everyone else—I was most attractive when I looked like myself. When I acted like myself instead of worrying about what everyone else thought of how I looked.

And now, standing here, ready to bare my fashion-designing and body-image soul to a crowd of my professors and peers, I felt just as strong as the first time I went rock climbing Except not on the outside. The outside wasn't important anymore.

A row of models finally appeared on the stage to thunderous applause—this was the fashion show equivalent of a curtain call. Each student designer had chosen the outfit that she felt best represented her collection and abilities, and chosen that as her final image.

The emcee, the dean of the fashion design school, stepped out to the podium and gestured to the models behind him. "Let's give these hardworking ladies one more round of applause." I joined in. I knew the long hours those girls worked sitting under makeup lights and then strutting unnaturally under stage lights. It was tough work making clothing look like art, no matter what size you were.

"Now, a very special addition to this year's program. We asked our design students to consider thinking outside the box in their design projects. And this year, we offered a specific assignment with an incentive. Project Real Woman is funded by the Body Image Awareness Council of the United States of America. The challenge was to transform the idea of fashion for a beauty industry that can often be narrow-minded both figuratively and literally."

The crowd chuckled, including the stick-thin models on stage. I knew full well from working with them that most of them weren't starving themselves—for most of them, being tall and thin was just as hateful as being heavier had been for me. They'd just found the one place where looking like that was accepted.

My stomach twisted with anticipation. I knew that my project was up first, because the students on tech were rolling in two humongous TVs. My project was entirely on video. If these thin model bodies were considered art, this crowd was about to get a blast from the past, a genuine Botticelli.

"Before we begin with our first entrant, fashion design program junior Catherine Mitchell—" I stood up from my chair right beside the stage and gave a little wave—"we have a very...insightful introduction from architecture student Nathaniel West."

My heart stopped. I knew he was here somewhere but I had told myself that I'd show my project and it would do its job. I wouldn't have to speak to him, or see him, at all.

Why the hell was he introducing the one project he'd discouraged me from doing? The one that he seemed to hate so much just a year ago at USC?

He stepped up to the podium and my stomach clenched at how good he looked. He was wearing a plain black suit with a white shirt and a pale blue tie. As much as I hated him, and as far down as I'd tamped down the feelings of love that had been just about to brim out of my mouth before I stormed from his house, they all came rushing back.

And God help me, he'd known exactly where I was sitting, because he flashed those puppy dog eyes at me before he started.

He cleared his throat.

"Good evening. My name is Nathaniel West. My friends call me Nate. That's for a very specific reason." He held up a small black remote control and clicked a button. The TVs behind him flashed on to the very same yearbook photo that I'd seen, sitting in Nate's living room a week and a half ago. Of the pudgy kid with neck fat and a jaw hidden by chub. He glanced back, then turned red and chuckled.

"That's me. At twelve years old. The only girl I could get to kiss me," his eyes flashed to mine, "was in a game of Seven Minutes in Heaven at summer camp. Kids made fun of me all the time. I didn't sit at anyone's lunch table, and I sat warming the bench on every sports team that would let me on."

He clicked again, and the picture changed to the next year's yearbook photo—pretty much the same. "I was fat, and school sucked, but at home, I was happy." He clicked a few more times, and a series of pudgy-Nate pictures scrolled over the screen, a bunch with his dad.

"When my parents got divorced, I got depressed. Really depressed. And I blamed the fact that I was fat. So I lost weight." He clicked to the picture of skinny Nate, a senior in high school. "But by the time I got to college, I'd realized that, surprise surprise, being skinny didn't fix anything." The crowd chuckled.

"But I was stupid. I was so stupid that I thought I should get big. But not fat." He paused for half a second, then clicked. "Buff."

That fourth bodybuilding picture came up, the one that looked mostly like MY Nate, the one I saw when it was just me and him and his body under my hands.

Oh, God. I couldn't think like this. For whatever reason, he was here and about to reveal his douchiness to everyone.

Except, before a project like this, where bigger models were the subject matter, it made absolutely no sense. That was everything he stood against.

"I even wrote articles for a website just for kids who wanted to be buff like me." The exact same articles I'd seen in his house scrolled past in rapid succession.

"I had skinny girlfriends. Sometimes I had buff girlfriends. They were all society's definition of hot." Pictures of Nate and various girls flew past now. Some wolf whistles sounded, and I rolled my eyes.

"And then at USC, one of the art magazines did a spread of plus-sized models, nude. And because of how sad I had been as a kid, and how much I had been taught that anything overweight turned into anything bad, I let what happened to me eight years before turn into the most hateful article I'd ever written."

Various phrases from the article zoomed onto the screen, ending with the one I thought was worst:*Big bones didn't make them like this, big meals did.*

The room was completely silent.

"The day that article came out, I was a hero in the gym. All my buddies clapped me on the back. And my girlfriend giggled because she was so the opposite of all the stuff that I thought was so very wrong. And I even got some comments telling me 'way to go,' on the site.

"But the next day, as often happens with these things, there was a side effect. A ripple. One of the girls in the photo shoot for that magazine? It was her first time posing nude." A photo of a girl with skin the color of chocolate and short, curly hair, probably a size bigger than me, in jeans and a sweater, filled the screen.

"This is Anna Hawthorne. She read my article. And what she had done, posing for that spread? Had taken all her courage. And she didn't have that much left to deal with the stupid opinions of jerks like me. That night, she tried to kill herself."

There were a few gasps in the crowd, but it was mostly silent.

"I felt awful. Of course, by then, there was nothing I could do. I sat with her in the hospital. I apologized. And I quit bodybuilding, because I didn't like what I had become when I was in that environment. I was arrogant, and I thought that the way people looked could tell me something about who they were.

"So I transferred here to a school in Philadelphia, hoping to escape it all. But I should have known, you can never escape your past. Almost as soon as I set foot on campus, I ran into the first girl who had ever made me feel good about myself, no matter how I looked." A photo of him and me came on the screen—one of the ones we'd snapped on a cell phone after rock climbing. "And I realized that she was the last girl I ever wanted to make me feel that way, too. I fell in love with her."

"But, once again, I made a really big mistake. I didn't tell her what a jerk I used to be about girls that had a little extra weight than your average praying mantis, and she found that article that caused Anna Hawthorne so much pain. And it caused her pain, too."

"But the truth is, from the moment I saw her again, I realized that not only do I not find the thinnest bodies the most attractive, but that what our bodies look like doesn't even factor into the equation. I love her just as much meeting her now as I would have if I met her two years ago, when she looked different."

"That girl's name is Catherine, and she's a really impressive fashion design student. I worked with her, I've seen her in action. She has incredible ideas, and I know that when she shows you this project, she will blow you away.

"And since she asked me never to talk to her again, I just want this opportunity to tell her, for the first and last time. I love you, Cat. Thank you for everything." His voice hitched at the end, and he sat left the stage and took a seat across the runway from me.

Shit. Shit, shit shit.

I'd had no idea. How could I? Anger and guilt roiled through me in equal measures. I should have let him explain, maybe. But it was too late now, and if my Real Women Project wasn't basically a big "fuck you" to...well...him, I didn't know what it was.

I swallowed the lump in my throat as I walked up the stairs to the podium, particularly aware of the hot lights shining on me. Sweat beaded at my hairline.

"Ah....thank you, everyone. And thank you, Board, for considering my entry." I cleared my throat. This was going to be harder than I thought. "A year ago, I weighed about sixty pounds less than I do today. I worked as a model, and I think I even shared the runway with some of these beautiful women behind me. I was in a horse-riding accident last spring break. My tibia was shattered, and now a rod and bolts replaces the solid bone that once was there. Ah...."

I shuffled my papers. Oh, Jesus. This was going to be ridiculous.

"I couldn't exercise, and I was on steroids. And I was depressed. So, in ten months, I gained about sixty pounds. And now I look like this. When I came back to school, the guy I'd been seeing dropped me like a bad habit. And I felt horrible.

"I was so depressed, it was starting to get hard to function. I saw a therapist, and she told me to get back into modeling—nude modeling. That's how I met Nate. But then...he hurt me. And I cried." I laughed, trying to hold back tears at that moment. "But then I got my act together, and realized that with or without him, or any guy, or any modeling gig in my life, I was just fine. I was still me, still lovable and worthy and attractive. No matter what I looked like."

"I didn't find any models for this project. Every model is me. Because this journey is mine, and I am a real woman."

The applause was ridiculously loud for just an introduction, and I was so embarrassed of the attention that I was relieved when the lights went down.

Joey had helped me settle on a slow, sexy track as a backdrop for the photographs, mostly because she thought it would be a good contrast to what people normally heard behind these things—it would make them slow down, and concentrate on the cards I held in front of each outfit.

The outfits themselves were gorgeous—a red satin evening gown, the flowy white blouse, the tweed suit with ruffles peeking out everywhere. Each design had been inspired by the architectural insights I got from Nate, almost without realizing it. Each design on a plain-colored background. And for each photo, I held up a simple white board sign with hand lettering:

The thing is
As much your words hurt my heart
I needed to see what an asshole you were
To realize that I was

Who I was
Worthy
Strong
Deserving.
Without you.
I am real. I am beautiful.

Even though I'd known what the last shot was, it surprised me when I saw it—me, sitting cross-legged in a chair in the sunlight. Naked, and holding the sign in front of my chest.

When the lights went up again, the applause was thunderous. And then, they got even louder. After a few seconds, Nate started the standing ovation.

I counted to ten before I stepped up to the microphone again.

"Thank you, so very much."

And that was about all I could take. I walked off the stage as quickly as I could without looking like a freak. I knew I was supposed to sit in my seat, but as the dean of the school said, "Next up, our second of three entrants in the Real Woman Project...." I passed my seat and just kept going.

I made it out into the hallway, a long empty space lined with trophy cases and speckled tiled floors. Even though the fluorescent lights were atrocious, at least it was light and open and cool. And I could breathe.

I couldn't decide whether I wanted to talk to Nate. But I did know one thing. I wanted to find out. The anger and panic and nervousness roaring through my ears must have blocked out the sound of his footsteps.

"My buddy runs sound."

I whipped around to face him.

Nate stared at his shoes, and shrugged, catching my eye for a second. "He got me that intro spot. I have no idea what he told the dean, but...yeah."

I just stared. My mouth dropped open, but I couldn't even begin to form coherent thoughts. Between the true story behind the article, and the reason he had actually come here to Philly, and the fact that he had said he'd loved me, and the way I'd called him an asshole via cardboard sign in front of thousands of our classmates...I didn't even know where to start.

"I meant every word," he said. "I know I was an asshole, but you have to believe me. Things are different. My attitude, and...me. I'm different.

And, for what it's worth, I do. Love you. I hope you heard that. Did you?"

It was all I could do to choke out, "Yes." My chest burned. My whole body burned. I loved him too. Why couldn't I get the words out? All I could do was look at him with a trembling lip.

Now he spoke so quietly, you could have heard a pin drop next to us. "Didn't I talk about us like we were a thing from our first date? I fell in love with you that first time we went out for burgers and dancing. I love our weird dates and your belly laugh and how you see beauty in everything. Except yourself. And I love being the one to help you get there. I love the way you daydream, I love the way you hold my hand. I can't stop thinking about the way you taste."

His voice dropped on that one. Like he was saying something holy.

But I still said nothing.

"Look, you said we weren't going to hang out, and I respect that. So I'll just...leave you alone. But...you were great. Really beautiful, Cat. Even though you called me an asshole, I'm really proud that I know you." He took five steps away, then stopped, and turned over his shoulder. Speaking to me, but not talking to me. "And just so you know—I wasn't going to tell you this, because it sound so stupid and self-centered and dramatic—"

"Just say it." My voice was a tangled whisper.

"I'm leaving. I'm going back to my dad's. My enrollment back at USC is still valid and I'm going to go to a satellite campus." He looked back down, facing away from me. "So. Goodbye."

He walked three, four, five steps back into the auditorium, where he knew I couldn't chase him, because the next project was being showcased.

And once again, I dissolved into tears, and texted Joey, who gave up her spot at the showcase and walked my sorry ass back to the sorority house.

Chapter 18

I lay wide awake in bed, thinking of everything. Finally putting all the puzzle pieces together in my mind. My head pounded with the post-crying jag I'd been on.

But there were no tears left, so I'd washed my face, brushed my teeth and hair, and climbed into bed under the covers. Joey asked if I was okay,and I just nodded numbly, shut out the light, and stared into the darkness.

And stared.And stared.

And couldn't sleep.And couldn't stop replaying his words over and over in my head.

He loved me. He had changed. I had changed.

This was stupid.

"This is stupid," I whispered as I grabbed my nearest pair of yoga pants and a sweatshirt that was huge, but warm and comfortable.

I punched the number for a cab service into my phone, noting the time as I did. One thirty-five a.m.

I didn't give a shit.

The cab came ten minutes later, the exhausted-looking driver informing me that the fee was double between one and five in the morning. I just handed him a twenty and gave him Nate's address, seven blocks away.

The whole ride over, I was on edge. A new energy rushed through me and suddenly it was clear as day. I had to kiss him, had to tell him over and over that I loved him, and that I was sorry, that I understood now. But most of all that I loved him.

I had one hand on the seat belt buckle and the other on the car handle as we pulled up. The cab had barely stopped rolling when I hopped out. I bounded up the steps, and had my fist ready to knock on the door, when it opened inward so fast it took my breath away.

But when I saw Nate on the other side, I was truly breathless.

"I was just—"

"I couldn't sleep, so I—"

The same awkward talking-at-once as our first date. In just eight weeks, everything had changed so much.

"I'm sorry," he whispered. "I'm so, so sorry." He stepped toward me, put a hand out as if to touch my face, and then let it drop.

I caught it on the way down, and held it to my chest. "I'm sorry, too," I said. His eyes flashed to mine, full of surprise and desire and hope.

And then, in one fast, breathless moment, we said it at exactly the same time: "I love you."

I couldn't have kept myself off of him if I tried. I threw myself at him, pressing tight against his body, and he responded with one arm around my waist and one hand in my hair. We stood there, our lips crushing together desperately, tongues exploring places they'd already memorized a thousand times. It didn't matter. I would never be able to get enough of him.

His strong hands, the ones I'd wished would never leave my body so many times, slid down my torso, gripping and squeezing and molding my body to his. And then, they were on my thighs, and in one smooth motion, Nate had hoisted me up so my legs hitched around his waist, never breaking our kiss. He stumbled backward, and fumbled for the key to his apartment.

I had no idea how my sweatshirt came off, or who kicked off shoes when, or whose hands frantically pushed down whose pants. I didn't care. It didn't matter. I needed Nate's hot, hard body against mine. In mine.

When we finally broke our kiss, I caught his earlobe between my teeth and told him as much. And then he groaned from somewhere deep inside, and laid me back on the bed, and ran his hands over every inch of my skin, following soon with his lips and tongue.

By the time he'd made it down to my stomach, leaving a hot, wet trail, I was writhing and desperate for him. "You are sweet, and delicious, and absolutely perfect."

"And you are a sex god," I whined, half giggling. "Never stop."

"I won't, if you tell me I don't have to. I meant it when I said you were the last girl I ever wanted to make me feel this way."

"What way?" I whispered, temporarily ignoring the need that pulsed through every muscle in my body.

"Like you'll always want me, no matter what." He slid back up and kissed me fully, slowly on the mouth, his warm breath mingling with mine and tasting sweeter than I'd ever remembered it.

"Now that I know you're not an asshole anymore....Unh." I moaned, as his mouth returned to my stomach, then down to my hips.

"And never will be again, I swear to you, Cat," he murmured just loudly enough for me to hear.

"Then yes," I said. "Always."

In an instant, his mouth was back on mine, and we were wrestling on the bed, rolling and straining and fighting to get even closer.

And when he finally, finally buried himself in me, his white-hot heat filling me with steady, insistent thrusts, his moans filling my ears and his tongue tracing patterns on my neck, and finally, finally, a melting heat burst through my entire body and I clenched around him again and again, I knew.

I was beautiful, and he was gorgeous, but the most amazing thing about us was how perfect we were together.

And that would always be the same, no matter what.

Acknowledgements

If I'd created the story you just read all by my lonesome, it would have probably sucked. Thankfully, I had a lot of help.

Giant hugs to my first readers and partners in crime, Lyla Payne and Paisley Grant. There's no one I'd rather share secrets and hatch plans with. Love you both.

Picture Perfect was my first project with Copyeditor Jim (Thomsen) who made an encouraging comment about the story with every update, and indulged me with a wink and a laugh on occasion, too. Oh, and the important stuff – great work with the grammar, spelling, and structure, Jim. You're like coffee and concealer for a girl who partied too hard last night. Thank you.

Thank you to my publicist, KP Simmon – you make magic happen. I'm madly in love with you, and I don't care who knows it.

Molly Hansen, my proofreader – those seven mistakes you caught would have been damn embarrassing – more for Copyeditor Jim than for me. Thank you.

Thanks to my friend Sarah, who had gone from thin girl to slightly-less-thin girl almost overnight, and advised me on exactly how rock climbing straps would cut into one's ass.

Rachel, Alexa, and Andy, thanks for reading and telling me how true this story rang for each of you – you all are beautiful.

Lastly, thanks to every single writer who was told that stories about people in college would never sell, and who wrote them and published them anyway. You gave me the confidence to put what I think is an important story out into the world, naysayers be damned. You're a brave bunch, and I'm proud to count myself among your ranks.

To everyone who read this and found a little bit of herself in Cat – thanks for loving this story and nudging it a bit farther out into the world, you bunch of stone cold foxes, you.

About the Author

Alessandra Thomas is a New Adult writer who swears she was in hertwenties yesterday. Since that's sadly untrue, she spends her time looking backon her college years fondly, and writing sexy stories about guys andgirls falling in love and really living life for the first time.

Whenshe's not writing, you can find her with a spoonful of ice cream inone hand and the newest New Adult release in the other.

Picture Perfect is Aless's first New Adult novel. She had so much fun writing it that it definitely won't be her last.